"And you know we're destined to be together forever.

"To be married, in fact... You've been told this by your voice that tells you when patients are really ill?"

"Perhaps married in time. But for now I just know we have to be together."

He groaned. Then she felt him roll from the bed. When he spoke his voice was harsh at first, then became infinitely compassionate. But she didn't want compassion. She wanted to be loved.

"Delyth, your voice is wrong. I'm very fond of you. But any relationship I form will be temporary. I told you—I travel light. When I finish here I'll move on, perhaps to America. And I'll go alone. I've tried full-scale relationships, but they just don't work for me."

"So you want me simply as a temporary lover?" she asked.

His reply was stark. "Yes," he said.

The silence between them seemed to stretch forever.

Gill Sanderson is a psychologist who finds time to write only by staying up late at night. Weekends are filled by her hobbies of gardening, running and mountain walking. Her ideas come from her work, from one son who is an oncologist, one son who is a nurse and her daughter, who is a trainee midwife. She first wrote articles for learned journals and chapters for a textbook. Then she was encouraged to change to fiction by her husband, who is an established writer of war stories.

Seventh Daughter
Gill Sanderson

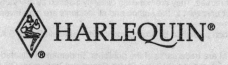

HARLEQUIN®

TORONTO • NEW YORK • LONDON
AMSTERDAM • PARIS • SYDNEY • HAMBURG
STOCKHOLM • ATHENS • TOKYO • MILAN • MADRID
PRAGUE • WARSAW • BUDAPEST • AUCKLAND

For my sister Wanda—with love

ISBN 0-373-51122-1

SEVENTH DAUGHTER

CHAPTER ONE

IT ONLY happened occasionally, which made it hurt more. And when it did Delyth was never wrong. She knew with an absolute certainty that the young man in the bed in front of her was dangerously ill. He might die before morning. And yet she could find little wrong with him.

It was midnight, and she had been bleeped to admit him to Gregory Ward—a surgical ward—from A and E an hour ago. He claimed his name was Birdie Jones, one of many young street-dwellers, and he'd been knocked down by a hit-and-run driver and brought in by ambulance. Apart from shock, abrasions and general bruising, he had a closed fracture of the radius—a broken arm.

'Don't think there's much seriously wrong with him,' the A and E registrar had cheerfully told her. 'We've put a plaster on his arm and patched him up. But keep him in for a couple of nights for observation. Feed him a bit, and then he can go out on the streets again.'

This was a hospital in the centre of London and there was something she had been told more than once. 'We provide medical care only. We cannot concern ourselves with social problems—we are not funded to do it.' Delyth knew this was a harsh but necessary doctrine.

Now young Birdie was in her care. She had clerked him carefully and followed the set procedures, keeping a close eye on blood pressure, pulse, abdominal signs. All was as expected. Although thin, he wasn't malnourished. But the knowledge had come with the strength of a physical blow. Birdie was in real danger. She checked all her findings again—what had she missed? Apparently nothing.

Delyth sighed. She was the humblest of doctors, a mere house officer. She had only qualified a few weeks ago. The correct procedure in case of doubt was to refer upwards, in this case to James Owen, the specialist registrar. But she knew James had been at work since six that morning, and he wasn't going to like being disturbed.

So far she hadn't met him. For the past fortnight he had apparently been away at a conference. Earlier today she had seen him in the distance, walking rapidly across the ward, white coat flying behind him. Even from a distance he gave an impression of energy, of determination. If it was possible to work out such a thing from just one glimpse, Delyth decided he didn't look a man who easily put up with fools. She sighed again.

She had been told that she could learn a lot from the senior nurses, that their opinion was always worth asking. So she asked Sue Ashton, the staff nurse in charge at night, what James was like. How would he react to being disturbed?

Sue was fortyish, married with three children who always phoned to wish her goodnight before they went to bed. She smiled amiably. 'Dr Owen? He's gorgeous,

Delyth. Sort of tall and lean and dark. He's a good doctor but he frightens me—he's all intense. Are you going to get him out of bed? I hope you've got a good reason.'

As Delyth thought of it, the conviction struck her again, stronger than ever. Birdie was ill. Whatever James Owen thought, she was going to call him. 'If he's in bed he'll have to get up,' she said. 'Can I use your phone?'

The phone was picked up practically at once. 'My house officer, Dr Delyth Price,' a dry voice said. 'Dr Price, you are talking to a very tired man. He is also stark naked, dripping wet from the shower and has a small whisky in his hand. He's on his way to bed. I hope this is important.'

It was an attractive voice. It was deep, with just a touch of humour to it which she suspected could easily become cutting. He didn't sound angry—yet.

The feeling flashed back. Birdie was ill, she knew she was right. But how to explain this to the SR?

'I've just admitted a young man from A and E. He's a road accident victim, just generally knocked about and with a fractured radius. He's in for observation.'

'What have you done for him?'

She detailed the necessary procedures, knowing that she had done everything properly.

'And there are no adverse signs? No cause for worry? Why have you called me?'

This was the difficult part. Drawing a deep breath, she said, 'I think I've missed something. I don't know what, but I have. So I called you.'

There was a pause. Then he said, 'You are a doctor

now, you know. There are decisions that you have to—
that you must make. You can't have your hand held
for ever.'

She could hear the iron in his voice, but didn't think
he was angry with her—yet. 'I'm making a decision.
I'm calling you.'

Now his voice was neutral. 'I'm on my way. Expect
me in about ten minutes.'

Gregory Ward was on the fourth floor and Delyth
waited near the entrance, expecting to hear the lift sighing upwards. But instead there was the patter of fast
feet on the stairs—he was running upwards. In the dim
light of the hallway she could see his open white coat,
and underneath it a white T-shirt, jeans, trainers without socks. He had come in casual clothes. He moved
well, like an athlete. Then, too quickly, he was up to
her, facing her.

He wasn't even out of breath. She felt his presence
and it was a shock to her. Inside her that distant voice
which was never wrong told her that this man would
have an effect on her. She was not sure what—it could
be a bad one. But she knew it, just as certainly as she
knew that Birdie was ill. The voice was never wrong.
Her life and this man's would be somehow intertwined.
The knowledge frightened her a little.

He was tall, lean, his hair dark brown and cut short.
Even when perfectly still, as he now was, there was
that impression of poised energy. His face was un-
smiling but he wasn't angry. She felt him assessing her,
waiting to give judgement. And she knew she wanted
this man's good opinion. Not just because he was her
senior. She wanted him to…like her. Delyth blinked.

She had never felt this way about a man so soon after meeting him.

'I don't really need to sleep,' he said wryly. 'What have you got for me?' Hearing him speak again, it was yet another thrill for her. She thought a voice was more affecting than simple good looks in a man. James's voice was deep, musical, with a tiny trace of a northern accent.

He held out his hand. 'Missed meeting you this morning, Dr Price. I'm sorry. I'm James Owen. I hope we'll work well together.'

'I'm sure we will,' she murmured. His handshake was firm but not forceful; it was their first bodily contact. The thrill of it ran through her.

Now he was closer she could see his eyes were dark grey. She saw them flick across her, noting her trim body, the black hair now tied tightly in a French plait.

'Don't tell me, you're Welsh,' he said.

'You get no points for that diagnosis, not when I have a name like Delyth Price.' She had to fight back.

'True. But doctors should never trust what is apparently obvious. You have a Welsh voice, and if there is a Celtic facial type then you've got it.'

This could turn into an interesting conversation, she thought. He might have thought the same, but instead he said abruptly, 'Let's have a look at this young man.' He yawned as he spoke, and when she remembered what he had already done that day she felt guilty. But, no, she was certain.

They strode down the ward corridor together, she conscious of how she had to step out to keep up with him. She went through Birdie's story and offered him her neatly written-out notes, telling him which tests she had conducted, what observations she had made. They reached Birdie's bedside.

'You seem to have followed every procedure absolutely correctly,' he said, 'and the results you have don't seem too worrying. Why did you call me out?'

'I've missed something,' she said flatly. 'I'm certain I have.'

He looked at her but said nothing for a moment. Then he shrugged and said, 'Well, let's take a look.'

His examination was as thorough as hers had been. And his results were exactly the same. There was nothing life-threateningly wrong with Birdie. 'Let's go to the doctors' room and have a coffee,' he said, after one last sharp look at the comatose form between them.

She poured him a coffee and he sipped, before saying, 'There was no need to call me out. Possibly there might be something wrong with your patient, but it isn't obvious from any signs.' He looked perplexed. 'Quite frankly, I'm surprised. I wouldn't have thought you were the kind of person to call for help unnecessarily. You seem both confident and competent.'

She thrilled to the compliment but there was nothing she could say. She still had that sense that something was wrong, but there was no way she was going to tell him now. She realised how easily he was letting her down: other registrars would have been angry. 'I'm sorry,' she mumbled.

'Don't be. You did what you thought best.' He yawned again. 'Bedtime but, don't forget, you can call me any time. Goodnight.'

He was gone, at the same speed with which he had

arrived. Again, he didn't take the lift. She went over to the window and watched him walking quickly across the outside quad. He turned to see her looking at him and raised an arm in farewell. She blushed as she waved back.

'How did he take being called out?' asked Sue as Delyth collapsed into a chair next to her.

'He took it very well. There was nothing there. I was wrong.'

'He didn't tell you off?'

'No. Perhaps he wanted to. Or perhaps he was too tired.'

'I've never seen him too tired to do what he really wanted,' said Sue. 'He *is* gorgeous, isn't he?'

Delyth was too fed up to lie. 'Yes,' she said simply. She didn't wish Birdie any harm but she wished Dr Owen *had* found something wrong with him. Then he might think better of her. Still…he wasn't angry with her apparently.

She could have gone back to bed. If there had been any serious change in any of the patients Sue would have rung her. Instead, she occupied herself with simple clerical tasks, then tried to doze in the doctors' room. At regular intervals she checked Birdie's condition. And at four-fifteen it happened. There was a sudden dramatic drop in his blood pressure. She looked, then fetched Sue to confirm her findings.

'If you don't send for the doctor, I will,' said Sue. 'This is an emergency all right.' So Delyth phoned him again.

His voice was sleepy. 'Owen here.' She had an unexpected vision of him in bed, but banished it at once.

'Sorry, Dr Owen, Dr Price here. That patient you saw—his blood pressure has dropped like a brick. It was OK five minutes ago, but it's going down fast.'

The sleepiness had gone. 'Right. Start phoning. We want a theatre, an anaesthetist, and we want them fast. Prep him as best you can and I'll be there in five minutes.'

After one last look at the now obviously ill Birdie, she went to do as James had asked. He arrived as she was putting the phone down. He was dressed just as before, but there were drops of water on his face and hair, and she realised he had dipped his head in a basin or under the shower.

Together they went to see Birdie, and once again he eased back the blankets and examined the bruises. Gently he palpated the abdomen. 'Concealed haemorrhage doesn't necessarily show itself at once. You can lose up to half your blood volume without any change in blood pressure. I'll bet this man has a ruptured spleen or something and he's been bleeding internally. Perhaps we should have had an ultrasound scan or a laparotomy but—I agree with you—there didn't seem any need to open the abdomen. You've got his blood cross-matched?'

'And ordered,' she said.

'Good. I've a feeling we're going to need it. Come on, let's go and scrub up.'

Birdie's spleen was indeed ruptured, and they had to take it out. She had seen and assisted in a splenectomy before, but had never seen it performed with such speed. He wasn't slapdash, but swift. And he gave her the chance to watch and to help with the more simple procedures. But finally it was finished, and Birdie was moved into the recovery room.

James stretched and yawned. 'A good job well done. I'm going to have a coffee before I get out of these greens. You need one too, I suspect.'

She peeled off her gloves and threw them into the bin. The excitement of the operation was now over, the adrenaline no longer pumping through her system. Suddenly a vast fatigue fell on her. 'I do need a coffee,' she admitted.

He poured two cups, passing her one. 'Now we have a problem,' he said. 'I'm supposed to be the expert, you the lowly house officer. But you spotted something that I didn't. You were absolutely certain there was something wrong, weren't you? Even when I said there wasn't.'

It was a difficult question, but she mumbled an honest answer. 'Yes,' she said.

'I want to know why and how you—' He broke off. With his forefinger he lifted her chin and looked at her. It was an intimate and exciting gesture, and she loved it. 'You're in no fit state to give thoughtful answers, are you? Have you arranged to sleep in tomorrow morning?'

She tried to conceal her feelings as she pointed to the window. 'The sun's shining—it *is* tomorrow morning. But, yes, Matt Dee, the other house officer will be in and I'll have a few hours in bed.' She was sorry when he took his finger away.

'Fine. I'm not going to ask now, but there are things I want to know. Have you been to the clubroom? Can we meet there for half an hour tonight if you're not doing anything else? Say about nine?'

It was a completely unexpected invitation. Also unexpected was her rush of pleasure at it. 'I'd like that.'

'Good. Now I'm off back to bed.'

Before she could go back to bed she had notes to write up. Then there was one last look at Birdie, and she was off across the sun-splashed quad to the residence. As she climbed wearily to her room she passed the kitchen shared by the five young doctors on her floor. A voice shouted, 'D'you want a cup of tea, night-owl?'

'Love one,' she called back, without bothering to stop.

Quickly she undressed, the habits of a lifetime making her put her discarded clothes away neatly. Then she pulled on her dressing-gown just as there was a knock on the door. 'Come in, Matt.'

Matt Dee was her fellow house officer on the consultant Michael Forrester's firm. The two had come to St Helen's Hospital together and had formed a friendship based on mutual need. Occasionally it occurred to Delyth that Matt would like their friendship to progress to something deeper, but for the moment she had enough to deal with. He was broad-shouldered and blond-haired—unlike her, he was a native Londoner.

'Busy night?' he asked her, handing her the mug of tea and sitting on her bed.

'Interesting. I've just finished assisting with an emergency splenectomy. I had to turn the SR out of bed twice.'

Matt whistled. 'James Owen? I did a ward round

with him yesterday. He's like a dynamo. Makes me tired just to watch him.'

'Any good?' asked Delyth, too casually.

Matt nodded. 'Knows his stuff and still has time for a word with every patient. Just cuts right down to essentials. I hope I turn out to be as good as he is.'

'So do I. Come on, Matt, off you go. You've got work and I need my beauty sleep.'

'Cast out of your bedroom again,' he said amiably, pulling himself to his feet. 'Delyth, a few of us are going to the Old Town Walls tonight—there's Singleton's Jazz Band playing. Fancy coming along?'

The Old Town Walls was a pub not too far away—she'd been there with a group once or twice before. She would have liked to have gone again, but remembered with a flash of pleasure that she was already meeting someone that night. 'Love to, but I'm meeting someone at nine. I'll try and catch the last few minutes, though.'

'See you there, then.' Matt sauntered out.

Clutching her tea, Delyth sat at the head of her bed. Her back propped against the wall, she looked round her tiny room. She supposed she was lucky to have it, to live here. St Helen's Hospital was in the centre—the very centre—of London. She could walk to Soho, Hyde Park, along the Embankment. It was very different from the tiny village she'd been brought up in north Wales.

She finished her tea, picked up a towel and walked along to get a shower. She would have preferred a bath, but knew that once in it she'd sleep. There was still tea in the pot when she returned, though the others had gone, and she helped herself to another mugful. Then she went back to her room to sleep.

But she didn't. This had happened before. There was a stage of fatigue so deep that she just couldn't sleep. The others had told her of it happening to them. So she sat up in bed and tried to write home. She hadn't had chance since sending the first scratched note when she had arrived. And she had so much to write about—everything was so different here. A mixed residence for a start. She picked up her pen. She would only need to write one letter, to her parents. She knew her mother would photocopy the letter and send copies to anyone likely to be interested. Bronwen Price was efficient. With seven daughters she had learned to be.

Delyth looked round the tiny room she had now lived in for a fortnight. Lived? She had done little else but sleep in it. It was clean, quiet; had bed, chair, desk, drawers, wardrobe, washbasin. Oh, and a window, but not a big one. It was painted a trouble-free white. She supposed it was all right. When she'd first moved in she'd allocated herself exactly three hours' home-making time. She'd bought a tray for the window-ledge, a set of pot plants and matching bright rugs for floor and bed. Fixed to the wall was her best buy, a four-foot square of plywood covered with cork tiles. On it were pinned pictures of her family, of the landscape round her village. Now the place felt like home.

'Dear all,' she wrote, 'Eight in the morning, been up all night and such a lot has happened. I'm so glad I came...'

It had been a definite decision. She'd spent most of her life in rural Wales, trained in a Welsh university, done her elective in a cottage hospital, working with Alun Roberts, the local GP, who had helped her so much in her ambition. But when she'd finally qualified she'd decided she needed something different. Probably she'd spend the rest of her life practising in Wales—why not see something of the rest of the world? So she had come to this central, metropolitan hospital.

So far she had been made very welcome. Her consultant, the head of her firm, the man technically in charge of her further training, was Michael Forrester. She'd only met him twice. He seemed caring, but he had an international reputation and spent much of his time on committees and travelling abroad. Mostly, she would learn from the two specialist registrars, James Owen and Peter Kenny. The other house officer she knew. He was, of course, Matt Dee.

Matt came from Essex and had trained locally. He knew London well, was streetwise in a way she was not. She'd happily accepted his offer to show her round in the odd few hours they could get away.

All this she wrote, in her usual chatty way. The hard work, the long hours, the difficulty in understanding some people—and those who pretended not to understand her Welsh accent. 'This morning I got the SR out of bed—twice,' she wrote. 'He didn't like it much, but in the end I was right. He seems...'

She laid down her pen. How did James Owen seem to her? Perhaps she was too tired to examine her own feelings. She merely wrote, 'His name may be Owen but I don't think he's Welsh.' Then she went to sleep.

Her last thought was that she was to meet him later. She was surprised at how happy it made her feel.

Because she had worked all night she was allowed a few hours' sleep, but she was back on the ward in the late afternoon and early evening. She was chatting to one of her patients who was about to be discharged, going through the seemingly interminable procedures that had to be followed and which were the special duties of the house officer.

She was getting a doctor's ear. There was the usual background noise to the ward—the rattle of feet, the hum of conversation, the tinkle of spoon on glass. And in the middle of it she heard a soft thump. A thump that shouldn't have been there.

Excusing herself, she darted into the next small room. On the floor by the bed lay an untidy pile of bedclothes, with a wizened head peering out of the top. Eighty-seven-year-old Mrs Ransome had fallen out of bed.

Calling for a nurse, Delyth knelt by the frail old lady. 'What am I doing down here?' Mrs Ransome asked, with some surprise. 'I was having a lovely dream.'

'Don't worry, Mrs Ransome,' Delyth said gently. 'Let's just make sure you haven't hurt yourself. You can get back to bed in a minute.'

With the shocked nurse's help she inspected Mrs Ransome for bruising or bleeding. Then she looked for fractures, looking especially at the wrist, hip and scaphoid bone—the one on the thumb side of the hand. Old people broke bones very easily, and the scaphoid bone was the one that fractured when people tried to stop a fall. But this time there were no breaks.

Gently, she and the nurse lifted Mrs Ransome back into bed then Delyth checked the old lady's temperature, blood pressure, pulse and respiratory rate. All were satisfactory. There was no need to assess the consciousness level on the Glasgow coma scale. Mrs Ransome never stopped chattering. She had apparently suffered no ill effects at all.

Delyth asked if side panels could be fitted to the bed, and wrote an account of the accident in Mrs Ransome's notes. She was given an accident form, which she completed and signed. Then she looked at her watch. Three quarters of an hour had passed. It was a busy life.

On the way back to her room she called at the canteen to buy a couple of sandwiches. She could eat them as she changed. She made herself the usual mug of tea and sat on her bed to consider. She was meeting Dr Owen in the Clubroom. It wasn't really what you would call a date, just meeting a senior colleague who wanted to get to know who he would be working with. After all, the consultant had taken her for coffee in the senior lounge. But she wanted to look—nice. There wasn't time to brush out her hair, but she tidied it. Then she put on black velvet trousers and a white silk shirt. A thin grey jacket in case it got cold later. As she set off she felt a throb of anticipation. Dr Owen was an attractive man.

She crossed the great quad, looking up at the red Victorian buildings on each side, then out of the main gate and into the busy London street. It still seemed strange to her, the hospital so close to the pulsing city centre. Down the road, past the vegetable stall that sold strange things she'd never tasted but had promised herself she soon would.

Affecting the casualness of a *habitué*—though she'd never been there on her own before—she entered the Saracen's Head. Bypassing the main bar, she walked down a dark corridor and pushed a door at the end under a sign saying NO SMOKING. This was the Clubroom—the unofficial meeting place of the medical staff of St Helen's Hospital. Technically it was a public room, but it was used almost exclusively by doctors and nurses. It was a comfortable room, dimly lit, with no piped music or arcade games. The paper and upholstery were dark red, the woodwork ornately carved. The landlord had a soft spot for doctors. St Helen's had successfully treated his wife for cancer.

Though Delyth was new to the hospital, there were a few people she recognised. And there in a corner was James Owen, standing to meet her. She didn't know what to make of the thrill she felt when she saw him, the dryness of her mouth and the shiver up her back. Probably nervous at meeting a senior man, she decided.

'Delyth, it's good to see you. It is Delyth, isn't it? And now we're off the ward you must call me James.' That gorgeous voice. Listening to it, it felt like being stroked by warm silk.

'You said the Clubhouse at nine,' she reminded him, then, hearing herself, added, 'Sorry, didn't mean to sound sharp.' What was wrong with her?

'No matter. You're here now. Sit in the corner there. What will you have to drink?'

'I'd like a white wine spritzer please, with chilled soda.' It was a drink to which Matt had introduced her, refreshing and only slightly alcoholic. As he went to order at the little window that opened into the main bar she glanced around again at the other people there. She had to admit it, there was an expression of curiosity on the face of a lady radiographer and frank envy from a gaggle of nurses.

She looked at James as he chatted to the landlord. He was still in jeans and a T-shirt. He looked like an athlete, she noted. There were no signs of a paunch. Too many male hospital doctors led disorganised lives, eating the wrong food at the wrong time, drinking too much alcohol and getting no exercise. By the time they reached thirty this life was having an effect. But not on James Owen. He looked well.

He came back with her spritzer and a beer for himself. 'One thing in the African bush I missed was good beer,' he said. 'There were imported wine and spirits, but only native beer. And it was horrible.'

She was interested. 'I didn't know you'd been to Africa.'

'Spent two years there, working in a rural hospital. No end of work, too. You have to move fast, but you learn a lot. I learned a lot of surgery there—but it's not a way to learn that I'd recommend to anybody.'

'Why not?' she asked curiously.

'No one to ask advice from, no one to consult. Professionally, you're alone. People think you have the answer and you know you don't.'

'So you weren't tempted to stay?'

The answer was long and drawn out. 'No-o.'

'Again, why not?'

He smiled at her. 'Look round a bit,' he said, indicating the rest of the room. 'This is the Clubroom. People come here to get away from the hospital—and they bring it with them. They're all talking about medicine.'

She let her ears take in the hum of conversations round her. He was right. 'We just need more beds...'

'Particularly tricky incision...'

'Not drug induced...'

'You're right,' she said. 'Aren't we a boring lot?'

There was a burst of giggling from the nurses in the corner, and a voice said, 'But the hem was far too low.'

'There you are,' Delyth said with some satisfaction. 'They're talking about dresses. Girl talk. It takes a woman to get away from work.'

He sniffed. 'I'm not convinced. I know that girl. She's a scrub nurse—she'll probably be talking about theatre gowns not ball gowns.'

They both smiled. She liked being with him, felt at ease with him. This surprised her. Usually she was a shy woman, rather in awe of her superiors. And James was an awesome man. So why did she feel so comfortable with him? 'You were going to tell me why you left Africa,' she reminded him. She wanted to know all about him—his history, what he liked, why he liked it.

He pursed his lips. 'Well, there was my career, of course. I want to make consultant in time, and, rather sadly, time in Africa doesn't seem to count for much. But, more important, I just got angry. I know I shouldn't have, I know it wasn't fair, I know a good doctor just accepts people as they are. But...'

He *was* angry, Delyth could tell. There was something about the set of his shoulders, the bleakness of his face. He was one of those frightening people whose voice got lower when they were angry—she was glad he wasn't mad at her. 'Go on,' she said.

She could see the conscious effort he made to relax. 'I didn't like the system there,' he said flatly. 'No, it's more than that. I just couldn't live with it. It's a fault in me. I should be able to distance myself from it, but I felt sympathy for the people involved.' He shook his head, as if to banish his bitter thoughts.

'Anyway, the last straw was when we had a lad brought in on an ox-cart. Name, Joseph. Problem, "pain in belly". It was a hell of a pain, too. I examined him. It wasn't a hard diagnosis—the lad had a hiatus hernia. I operated at once and sent him back to the ward, thinking I'd done a good job. Compared to ours, the wards were primitive—the rain used to rattle like fury on the tin roofs. But the staff were willing and competent. We were training them. Joseph was fine the next day. Told me he'd like to be a nurse or a doctor if it could be possible, and I encouraged him.

'Three days later I had to go to a village nearby to take a clinic. When I came back Joseph was gone. His mother had brought him in but his father had taken him out. There was nothing the staff could do. The father said they had no business interfering with a family matter.'

James paused and drank deeply from his glass. 'Did you ever see him again?' Delyth asked gently.

'I certainly did. A week later he was brought back again, weak, emaciated, his temperature sky high. I looked at the incision I'd made. Somebody had pulled off the dressing and smeared it with all sorts of muck.

The infection had gone too far. In spite of massive antibiotics, he died two days later. It turned out that some local healer type had said that the problem was devils, and that he would scare them out of the belly. He took off my dressing, smeared on his own, and Joseph died.'

'Even in England people believe in some odd things,' she pointed out.

'Don't I know it. People read their horoscopes and believe in them. Medicine's affected too. There's an entire army of con artists, offering cures for what can't be cured. Fake faith healers. Loonies who wave crystals over you and divine your illness. People with the *power*!'

Delyth was beginning to feel slightly apprehensive. His obviously sincere anger worried her. She didn't entirely agree with everything he'd said, and she suspected she was shortly going to have to tell him so.

He turned to smile at her, his sombre expression gone. 'I'm sorry to get all agitated,' he said. 'It doesn't happen very often. Now, what I'm really interested in is how you saw something that I missed this morning. You were absolutely certain that young Birdie was ill, weren't you?'

'I…thought so,' she said weakly.

'But you did every possible test, and so did I. There was no indication at all. We all know that ruptured spleens often don't present straight away—that's part of the trouble. But you knew. How?'

The trouble was, she knew his interest was absolutely sincere. He *did* want to know, if necessary to learn from her. As he looked at her he moved nearer.

She could feel the warmth of his body, his muscular forearm grazing hers. She liked him being so close, but she knew that what she was about to say would anger him. He hated what he called superstition.

'I just knew,' she offered. 'Call it woman's intuition.'

He shook his head decisively. 'Not good enough, Delyth. You weren't being intuitive—whatever that might be. You were absolutely certain. I want to know why.'

He frowned when she hesitated. 'I'm hoping to learn from you, Delyth. I like to think that I'm willing to learn from anyone. A doctor who thinks he knows everything is a positive danger.'

She had to try. 'I will tell you,' she said, 'but, please, don't tell anyone else. And don't laugh at me, and don't get angry at me.'

'Don't laugh at you and don't get angry at you? This is getting more and more intriguing.'

She sighed, thinking of what he had said about superstition. 'You'll think this is a Welsh old wives' tale, and I suppose it is. It doesn't happen very often. Sometimes I just…know that someone is seriously ill. I can feel it and I'm absolutely certain. And I've never been wrong. It's not the medical evidence—it's something from deep inside me.'

She paused, then looked at him accusingly. 'You're trying not to laugh. Or you think I'm a silly little girl.' She searched his blank face.

'A part of me thinks that,' he admitted. 'Quite a big part. But there was some proof. You diagnosed Birdie so I have to take you seriously. Tell me about another occasion it happened.'

She thought. 'Sometimes—often, in fact—it's obvious. The doctor in charge already knows. It's just that I know before I've read the notes or examined the patient. Once, when I was a student, I was sent to a local hospital to observe. I was in A and E and it was Saturday—we were very busy. A girl was brought in, triaged and put in a cubicle. The nurse who saw her thought her case was serious but not life-threatening. I knew it was life-threatening. I tried to tell the doctor, but he told me not to be so silly. He was madly busy, had serious cases to see to. And he had. The girl died. She had a brain haemorrhage. There was no way of telling, but I knew.'

The horror of that night was still with her. It could be heard in her voice. He put his hand reassuringly over hers. 'Remember, Delyth, we're not gods. We do the best we can, but some we lose.'

He may as well have the full story, she thought. 'Now I'm going to annoy you,' she said. 'You know the seventh son of a seventh son is supposed to have magic powers?'

He nodded. 'Yes. It's a superstition I've heard.'

'Well, I'm a seventh daughter. And my mother was a seventh daughter too. Now you can laugh.'

Shaking his head, he said, 'I'm not going to laugh. I'm impressed. But I'm not going to believe you either. There was a famous case of a horse who could count. Show it two cards, one with the figure five and one with three on, and it would stamp its hoof eight times on the floor. Its owner—and other people—believed implicitly that it had read the cards. But what really happened was that the horse was watching its owner, and it saw him tense after the eighth stamp. It reacted to that subtle signal, and the owner never realised what was happening.'

'I'm not a horse,' she said.

'There are doctors who can tell what's wrong with a patient just with one look. It's not instinct, just lots of little clues they've picked up without realising. You've got that ability, but you've got it early. In time you'll be a brilliant diagnostician.'

Well, he hadn't laughed at her. His theory was a good one, but she still felt he was wrong. No matter, now they could carry on as... How were they going to carry on? she wondered.

He finished his beer. 'D'you want another drink? I've taken up your time. You might have other plans for tonight.'

She'd really like to sit here and talk to him. But they'd only just met—she wouldn't be too forward. Still, she was certain she didn't want to part from him.

'I'd better not have another drink here. I've been invited to go to the Old City Walls with a group of young doctors. There's a jazz group there and I'd like to hear them.' She paused a moment, hoping. 'You could come if you liked.'

'If I liked?' He was teasing her.

'I'll rephrase that. I'd be glad of your company tonight and I'm sure everyone else would. Please, come.'

'I'd love to,' he said. 'Let's go.'

She was glad to sit down when they got to the pub. She thought of herself as a fit country girl, but James walked like one possessed. He had long legs, was a fast mover. When she mentioned it he slowed down—to just above a normal fast walk. 'Sorry,' he apologised. 'When I get time I do some running.'

Like all jazz pubs it was crowded, noisy and cheerful. She was squashed into a corner with Matt and others she vaguely knew. James got on well with everyone there, but she noticed a certain amount of deference to him. He bought a round of drinks, and she was interested at one stage to hear him telling Matt about the drum beating he used to hear in Africa.

When the band had played its last number, Matt and his friends decided to stay on. But Delyth told them she was tired and was going home. James offered to walk her back.

'This is so different from the silence at home,' she said as they paced through the London streets, still vibrant with night life. 'At this time most of my village is in bed.'

'Do you like London? Not too much of a culture shock?'

'Medicine here is a bit different,' she said cautiously. 'I sometimes think I ought to be a social worker as well as a doctor. And sometimes I think I should be a linguist too.'

'But what about the city itself?'

'I love it. It's so big and there's so much to do. It's so alive. I know I'll never see all I want to.'

They walked on in silence for a few moments. She noticed he'd moderated his pace and felt vaguely pleased. 'I've been in London since I was eighteen,' he said, 'apart from the two years I spent in Africa.

Would you like me to show you something of the city—say on Saturday morning? I've looked at the roster. I know you've got a couple of days off.'

She was rather intrigued that he'd bothered to look up her off days. 'I've already arranged to go out with Megan, my sister on Saturday morning,' she said, 'but I'd love it if you'd come with us.'

He seemed rather taken aback by this. Only after a moment did she realise that he'd wanted her to himself. 'Wouldn't I be in the way?' he asked.

'Not at all. Megan would love to see you. The thing is...where were you thinking of taking me?'

He shrugged. 'London is full of places. I thought Covent Garden, maybe, or a walk in a park if it was fine, perhaps down the Mall.'

She would have liked all those things, but Megan had work to do. 'I've arranged with Megan to meet in the British Museum.'

'The British Museum!'

'Yes, well, Megan likes looking at the stone carvings there—and so do I. But don't come if you don't—'

'Stone carvings? Just a minute—is your sister Megan Price the sculptor?'

Delyth was rather pleased he had heard of her. 'Yes, as a matter of fact, she is.'

'Good Lord. I had no idea. I'd really like to meet her.'

They were now in the quad of the hospital. He walked her over to the residence, and she stopped outside. Formally, she said, 'I've enjoyed the evening and your company, James. I won't invite you in because I'm tired.'

'I've enjoyed the evening, too, Delyth. I don't think I've ever had a house officer like you. Shall we meet here at ten on Saturday morning?'

He bent to kiss her briefly, like a friend. 'Goodnight, Delyth.'

He watched her as she walked into the residence lobby, then turned to go. She started up the stairs then peered back round the corner. He was walking away, fast again. James was driven.

She undressed and prepared for bed. Then she thought about the kiss. It had been friendly, no more than that. She thought she wanted more. James had affected her more than any other man she'd ever met. But she didn't know what she meant to him.

CHAPTER TWO

DELYTH enjoyed it, but life as a house officer was hard. The idea was that she learned on the job. Instead of listening, watching and questioning as she had as a student, now she had to make decisions. At times she was unsure.

She started next morning by doing the bloods, taking specimens and sending them for analysis. Often it was easy, sometimes it was not. There were more than a few drug addicts on Gregory Ward, most of them having injected themselves so often that their veins had just shut down. If necessary she could call on the services of a professional phlebotomist, a middle-aged woman who did nothing but tour the wards, taking blood. But Delyth wanted to be able to do the job herself so she persevered.

There was the usual mass of paperwork. Then there was time for some real medicine. She had to clerk the day's intake of patients. She was soon reminded that there was nothing minor about any procedure in hospital.

Wendy Webster, a rather stout woman aged about fifty, had come in for the most minor of operations. She was to have a phlebectomy, her varicose veins taken out. As with all non-life-threatening operations there had been a waiting list, but Wendy's appointment had now come.

'I've had to wait an awful long time, Doctor,' Wendy complained mildly, 'and I've been feeling very tired lately. D'you think I'll feel better afterwards?'

'You should move a lot more comfortably,' Delyth said. 'We'll just have to see.' She had been warned against promising patients that all their problems would be solved after their operations.

After writing down the basic information Wendy offered, Delyth examined her patient's legs. The veins were prominent, and Delyth performed a Trendelenberg test, raising each leg to drain it and then applying tourniquets so that when Wendy stood she could remove them and note the level at which the vein filled with blood. Then she identified the perforators in the veins by placing the Doppler probe over the calf and compressing the flesh until she could hear the hiss of venous blood. Her conclusions were carefully noted.

'We'll finish with a general look at you,' Delyth said. 'It would be a pity to miss anything.' She carried on with her overview examination, checking and noting Wendy's respiratory, neurological and cardiovascular systems. For her age and weight, Wendy was in reasonable shape. There seemed to be no reason she shouldn't have a general anaesthetic.

'Now, if you'll just slip down your nightie, I'll check your breasts,' Delyth said finally. She glanced at the notes. 'I see you've never had a mammogram or a smear test.'

'I've had enough trouble with my legs,' Wendy said firmly. 'I don't want to spend all my time at the doctor's. My GP suggested it, but I told him I didn't want to bother.'

This was not an uncommon reaction, Delyth knew. Too many patients felt that if they had one illness they were mysteriously prevented from contracting another. 'It's always a good idea to have a test,' she said gently. 'It gives you peace of mind. Do you ever check your breasts yourself for lumps?'

Wendy didn't. She indicated that she felt it wasn't quite ladylike.

'Never felt any pain there? No discharge, no alteration in shape or size?'

'Nothing, Doctor. Apart from my legs, I'm fine.'

Carefully, Delyth palpated each breast in turn. And there, in the left breast, was a lump—with that unmistakable gritty feel that suggested cancer. She managed not to let the dismay she felt show on her face.

There were other questions and tests to follow. She felt the lymph nodes in Wendy's armpits, asked about breathlessness, loss of weight, palpated the abdomen.

'There'll be someone else to see you in a while Wendy,' she said finally. 'You can pull up your nightie. That's all for the minute.'

'I'll be glad when these veins are done,' Wendy said. 'Then I can start enjoying life again.'

'That's the spirit,' Delyth agreed.

Earlier on, Peter Kenny, the other specialist registrar, had come on the ward. He had nodded to Delyth in his usual rather abrupt way and asked her for the case notes on a patient. Now she found him in the doctors' room, drinking coffee and writing up his examination.

'I've just clerked Wendy Webster,' Delyth said. 'She's on your list for a phlebectomy tomorrow.'

'Quite so. Do you want to assist?'

'There's a lump in her breast. I'm pretty sure it's cancerous.'

Peter put down his pen. 'I see. What tests have you done?'

She shook her head. 'Just the usual examination. And I certainly haven't told her what I suspect. Wendy thinks she's here for a simple operation on her legs. She's bound to wonder what's wrong if we start messing round with the other end of her.'

'That's true. Well, I'd better come and have a look and we'll think about a mammogram and a fine needle aspiration biopsy. Then we'll decide if we want an oncologist to see her.'

Delyth nodded. Once they had an X-ray of the lump and had taken a tiny sliver of it for laboratory examination, they'd know what they had to do. '"In any examination always check the breasts",' she quoted. 'I certainly know why now.'

'Finding something you don't expect is always a shock. I'm afraid you'll get used to it, though.'

Peter had the reputation of being competent but rather distant. Delyth was finding him sympathetic.

She didn't see much more of James. He waved to her once when he was visiting someone in the ward, but she was busy herself and had no good excuse to go and speak to him. As ever, he was moving fast. She remembered her earlier ideas about him—he was driven.

'What was James doing on the ward?' she asked Staff Nurse Ashton, well aware that her apparent casualness wasn't fooling the shrewd sister at all.

'Just wanted to check on Birdie Jones's condition,' Sue said comfortably. 'I'm surprised he didn't come over to ask you about him.'

'I was trying to get in touch with Wendy's husband. He's left a daytime contact number, but his firm couldn't find him. They seemed to think it was my fault.'

'It's always the doctor's fault. Anyway, James had to rush off to a clinic at one of the other hospitals. Good-looking man, but he doesn't seem ready to settle down yet, does he? I've seen him with one or two ladies, but nothing ever came of it.'

Delyth recognised that this was a delicate and well-meant warning. 'Perhaps he just hasn't yet found the right woman,' she suggested.

'Perhaps.' Sue wrinkled her forehead and rubbed her eyes with her palms. 'There was something I heard about him before he went to Africa... I can't remember—not a scandal, a tragedy. I was away at the time so it didn't concern me.'

'You can't remember?' asked Delyth, trying to conceal her interest.

'It'll come back to me. Mind you, there's always gossip in hospitals, and most of it is untrue.'

'Isn't it just?' said the disappointed Delyth. She wanted to know as much about James as possible.

Saturday morning came with warm, early September weather. Delyth dressed in jeans, a dark shirt and flat shoes. Any museum trip with her sister was likely to involve lots of walking.

It didn't surprise her that James wasn't waiting for

her, standing in the sun or sitting on a bench. Instead
he was pacing along the side of the quad, looking up
at the fine red brickwork. Like her, he was dressed
casually, in jeans, polo shirt and a light jacket. For a
moment she had time to study his face before he noticed her. There was a bleakness there, she thought,
almost a sadness. She wondered why as she walked to
his side. 'I'm not late. I'm exactly on time.'

His face changed when he looked at her, obviously
pleased to see her. 'True. And I suspect you're never
unpunctual.'

He took her arm and turned her towards the gate.
'Let's go. There are lots of ways of getting about central London—taxis, the Tube, buses, even bikes—but
the one most people seem to forget is walking.'

'I like walking,' she told him, 'but not always at
your rate.'

'Sorry. Sometimes I forget.' They strode off together. 'It's only fifteen minutes to the British
Museum.'

There weren't quite as many tourists outside the museum as there had been in high summer, but still the
broad steps were covered with them, chattering in a
dozen languages and industriously photographing each
other. Delyth and James threaded their way upwards.

Delyth had arranged to meet her sister in the shop
just inside the entrance; as ever, Megan had bought a
dozen postcards. The two girls were recognisably sisters, even though Megan was ten years older than
Delyth. Her dark hair was cut fashionably short and
she was dressed strikingly as always, all in black with
a barbaric silver necklace. There was a large notebook

and pencils stuffed into the pocket on her thigh. Megan never moved far without her sketchbook.

After kissing her sister, Delyth introduced James. The two looked at each other warily. 'You're older than Delyth,' Megan said abruptly.

He smiled. 'I like big sisters who look after little sisters,' he said. 'I'm only about eight years older.'

Megan relaxed. 'I'm sorry, I can't get over treating her as an innocent child in the evil city. I'm pleased to meet you.' She waved her hand in one of her imperious gestures. 'Is there anything you particularly want to see here?'

'Everything. It's terrible to admit, but I've never been here before. I visit all the art galleries and the V and A regularly, but never here.'

'You'll never take it all in in one visit. You need to come regularly. The Assyrian statues—'

'Why did *you* particularly want to come?' Delyth broke in. 'You said there was something you needed to look at.'

'I've been commissioned to do a bronze for the entrance hall of a company that trades a lot with Egypt and the Middle East. I've come looking for inspiration.'

'We'll follow you,' James said. 'And when you want to stand and think a while then we'll wander on.'

'Yes,' said Megan thoughtfully, 'that's a good idea.'

After strolling through galleries devoted to twentieth-century art, they eventually came to one that featured early art from Saudi Arabia. Here they stopped. Delyth could tell that Megan was excited by what she saw. Her eyes were fixed on a bronze ibex, her replies to their questions shorter.

James winked at Delyth. 'Why don't we wander on round and meet you later?' he asked Megan. 'You obviously want to study this for some time.'

'Mmm? Sorry, oh, yes,' mumbled Megan. 'In the café in about an hour, then.' As they walked away she had pulled out her sketchpad and was already slashing the first bold strokes across it.

Delyth sighed with exasperation and fondness. 'She's always like this. In fact, all my sisters are like it. They're all artists of some sort and they're all single-minded. She doesn't mean to be rude.'

'I didn't think she was being rude. I like people who know what they want.' After a while he asked, 'So, why aren't you an artist too?'

She shook her head decisively. 'Never any chance of it. I like a lot of the things my sisters like, but I knew medicine was for me from when I was very young. I never even thought about anything else.'

'Interesting,' he murmured. 'I didn't make my mind up till later.'

She was enjoying herself. He was a good companion to walk round a museum with, always ready to stop and talk about what they were viewing. They moved to the stairs and paused to look at a magnificent collection of bronze plaques. He frowned as he read the account of what they were seeing.

'I remember these,' he said. 'They were originally cast about a hundred miles from where I worked.'

She was surprised. The thought didn't seem to please him.

'Delyth, how could the people who created these not progress further?'

'You're thinking about that boy who died,' she said. 'You know doctors can never ask why people apparently get themselves into trouble. We help when we can. Everyone's flawed—we have to expect that and include ourselves.'

'I know, Delyth, I know! It just…angers me at times. That boy's death was an unnecessary waste of a life. And all through superstition.'

'People need to believe,' she said, 'and it's not up to us to tell them what to believe. Come on, let's go and look through here.'

Five minutes later he had apparently forgotten the folly of superstition and was fascinated by the intricate pattern on the side of a primitive bowl. She liked him for his enthusiasm. Too many of the older doctors she had met cultivated a world-weary attitude, probably as a way of dealing with the problems they saw. Not James. As she had told herself before—he was driven.

Her legs were weary before his were, and she had to remind him that they were to meet Megan in the café. She waved to them as they entered. James fetched a tray of sandwiches and tea and the three of them sat in a corner.

Megan's preoccupation had disappeared. Waving a sandwich, she told them happily that she had made a dozen rough sketches and that a basic idea was emerging. 'It's based on that carving of a boat I saw,' she told them. 'It was an incense burner. But it'll be quite different. Now I know where I'm going I can relax.'

She turned to look at James more closely. With a

sinking feeling Delyth realised that Megan had decided that it was time to turn all her attention on the slightly older man her little sister had brought along. 'Did you enjoy your visit, James?' she asked.

'Very much so. It's now on the list of places I'll visit regularly.'

'That's good,' said Megan. 'Which places in London don't you visit regularly?'

He wasn't upset by this odd question. 'Parliament,' he answered promptly, 'especially the House of Commons. It's full of people apparently not getting anything done.'

'You believe you could do better?' Megan pressed him.

'Sometimes I feel I could cut a lot of unnecessary talk and get on with things. It's a doctor's fault. We all think that we can do better than everyone else.'

Delyth decided to try to save him from a further inquisition. 'That's because all the young nurses and doctors look up to you and think you're marvellous,' she said.

He sighed mournfully. 'If only that were true. A man can dream.' He looked at his watch. 'Ladies, I have to go. There's work waiting for me and I know you two have a lot to talk about.' He stood and offered his hand. 'Megan, I've really enjoyed meeting you. I hope to see you again some time.'

Megan smiled the sweet smile which, Delyth knew, hid a quickly calculating mind. 'It could be sooner than you think,' she said. 'I'm having a little party tonight. Delyth's coming. Would you like to come too? Nothing formal, just a couple of dozen friends.'

Delyth felt his questioning look on her. 'Do come,' she said. 'We could share a taxi. I'm *not* going to walk in my best outfit.'

'Then I'd love to come.'

'Arrive about nine,' Megan said, obviously pleased. 'Delyth knows the address—it's on top of Crouch Hill.'

'Looking forward to it.' He rested his hand on Delyth's shoulder a moment and then he was gone, striding rapidly between the tables. The two sisters watched him in silence.

Delyth poured herself some more tea. 'Are you going to do the big sister act?' she asked with a grin. 'Either tell me off or ask me if there's anything in it. You'll have to report on me to Mum, you know.'

Unusually, Megan wasn't ready with an opinion. She seemed preoccupied. 'What do you read in his face?' she asked.

Delyth was instantly wary. Her sister was good at faces. She was knowing rather than tactful. Once she had sculpted the head of a politician in bronze. The politician had loved it, but a reviewer had pointed out that it showed every flaw in the man's character. 'I don't know,' she said. 'What do you read in his face?'

As Delyth had known, Megan wasn't having this. 'I asked first. Tell me about his character.'

'I've really only known him a few days. He'll be one of the bosses I'll be working with most regularly for the next six months. He's very competent and I think I'll learn a lot from him. He works fast and hard and expects everyone else to do the same.'

'I'll bet he works hard,' Megan said. 'Go on, tell me about his face.'

'He's fit,' Delyth went on. 'I never see him still for long. His face is pleasant, not traditionally good-looking but all right. Nice curved mouth and good teeth but doesn't smile much.' She hesitated. 'He...attracts me more than any man I've ever met.' There. She had said it.

'What about his eyes?' Megan asked, ignoring Delyth's confession.

'Well, they're grey, I suppose, but—'

'Haven't you ever heard that the eyes are the windows of the soul?' Megan asked impatiently. 'You're sounding like a doctor, not a woman. What do his eyes tell you?'

'I'm both doctor and woman,' Delyth said sturdily, 'and happy to be both. Now, you tell me about his eyes.'

'You're working too hard,' Megan muttered. 'I suppose I can't blame you, it's a family trait—we're all single-minded.'

Delyth eyed her sister with some irritation. 'You're getting annoying,' she said. 'Come on, say what you have to.'

'There's something hidden in his face. It's very interesting. I'd love to do a bust of him. But there's something he's not telling people. He goes to a lot of trouble to hide it, but it's there.'

'You can't tell all that just from looking at his face,' Delyth said. 'You're making it up.'

'I've done it before,' Megan said flatly, 'and I've been right, haven't I?'

Delyth thought a minute. 'Yes,' she said.

*   *   *

She went back to her room at the residence, worked for a while and then slept for a couple of hours. She was learning to sleep whenever she could. Often there wasn't the chance.

For a small treat she allowed herself time for long, luxurious preparations. She had a scented bath instead of a shower, rinsed her hair and sat in her room for the long process of drying it. While she did so she listened to the *Messiah* on her CD player, singing along with the contralto part—indeed, all the parts.

It wasn't hard to decide on a dress—she didn't have all that many. She decided she'd wear— The phone rang.

'I liked your sister,' the instantly recognisable voice said, 'and I'm looking forward to the party.'

She'd only known him for a few days. He was a colleague and becoming a friend, but was it normal to feel such a burst of pleasure at hearing his voice unexpectedly? 'James?' she asked.

'I'm causing trouble, as ever, because I left before making those social sounds that are so important. It's every woman's question. What shall I wear?'

She giggled. 'All women have a different answer to that.'

'Well, I've got my penguin suit, but I don't think it will be that formal. I've got the clerical grey interview suit too, but I doubt that is the right thing. I'm lost.'

She told him, 'Megan has a wide variety of friends and some of them will be wearing suits. Others will be in jeans. You'll just have to decide.'

She heard him sniff. 'If you gave me that kind of briefing on the ward I'd give you a real telling-off.

You're supposed to make my life easy. What're you going to wear?'

Time to make her mind up. 'I've got a dark blue dress.'

'Right. Grey goes with blue. I'll wear a light grey suit. Should I bring a bottle?'

'Doubt if it'll be that kind of party. But you could take a bunch of flowers if you like.'

'Or descend from a helicopter with a box of chocolates. You know, social life in Africa was much simpler. Shall I knock on your door about half past eight?'

This was unexpected. She could meet him downstairs but... 'Fine,' she said. 'I'll be ready.'

'I'll order a taxi.'

She'd made her mind up the moment he'd asked. She'd wear the blue dress. Now she took it from her wardrobe and looked at it dubiously. It certainly suited her. It was just that it... attracted attention.

Her hair was brushed till it shone, then she tied it back with a blue scrunchie. She rummaged through her underwear drawer. With this dress she couldn't wear her customary sensible things. She pulled on a pair of white silk French knickers—she didn't want the lines of leg elastic showing through. For a moment she considered going without a bra, but knew it wasn't a good idea. Her breasts were high and firm but... She put on a flesh-coloured bra which contained rather than supported. It was still summer—she wasn't going to wear tights.

He'd be here in fifteen minutes. She slipped into the dress, zipped it up and looked at herself. It was of blue silk, high-necked at the front but with a V-back and sleeveless. There was a slash to the right thigh. Her sister Bethan had bought it for her as a twenty-first birthday present. She remembered when she had first shown it, it had silenced all the family. 'Only a young girl could wear a dress like that,' her mother had said.

The skirt was lined, but even so it clung to her body like a second skin. She brushed it down, sat again and put on just a little more than her usual minimal make-up. Her green eyes were a good feature—she'd emphasise them a bit more.

Finally, she was finished. The 'Hallelujah Chorus' roared out of her CD player. She smiled and joined in. There was a knock at the door.

James looked well in a light grey suit. With it he wore a darker grey shirt and a tie in dull rich colours— maroon, amber, navy. And his expression was startled.

'Delyth, you look...' He swallowed. 'You look wonderful.'

'I *can* dress up when I want,' she pointed out. 'I don't spend all my time in flat shoes and sensible clothes to go with a doctor's white coat.'

'But your hair! It's right down your back. I'd no idea it was so long. It's glorious.'

She felt pleased at the compliment. 'Thank you. It's my one feminine concession. The rest of my life is concentrating on being a good doctor—this is my bit of wildness. But it can get in the way. Sometimes I think I'll cut it off.'

'Don't! It would be a tragedy.'

She decided to change the subject. 'Anyway, you've

made an effort, too. I've never seen you look so—debonair.'

'What a lovely word. Remind me to look it up.'

Stepping back from the door, she waved him in. 'Come in. There's not a lot of room but you can sit on the bed.'

He came in, sat as directed and looked round. 'Why did I know your room would be like this?' he asked. 'All it is is a box, and yet you've turned it into a home. I've got a hospital flat round the corner. Take the clothes and books out of it and there'd be nothing of me left.'

'You need a good woman,' she said, then blushed. 'Sorry, didn't mean that.'

He smiled at her ferociously. 'One day I'll quote that back to you.'

She thought it would be a good idea to change the subject. 'What's that in your hand?' she asked. It was a small box, wrapped in dark red paper.

He shrugged. 'I'm not taking a bottle or flowers. It's just a little gift for my hostess.'

'What is it? I've got an enquiring mind.'

'You're just nosy,' he told her. 'Wait and see.'

As it was Saturday night, those in the residence who weren't working were certainly going out. The entire building seemed to be full of bodies, rushing to the bathroom, ironing clothes, demanding to borrow scent or shoes. They were bound to be noticed. Delyth had thought of this. Once she would have asked him to meet her in the quad or even on a street corner. Now she was happy to have him call for her. She knew hospital gossip was like wildfire. So what? Never before in her medical career had she caused any kind of interest. She could do so now.

Crouch End was an interesting district. Their taxi took them up the steep hill so all of London lay displayed below them. Delyth liked the variety of restaurants and the walk along the old railway route to Highgate. The taxi drew up at a large Victorian house, converted into four flats. She explained that Megan had a flat, as well as a studio at the back of the house which had been converted from the old coach houses.

'I should have asked,' James said. 'I saw Megan wasn't wearing a wedding ring so I presume she's not married. Does she have what is usually called a partner?'

'Not at the moment,' Delyth said, 'though she has had several.' She knew she sounded both defensive and rather prudish.

He spotted it. 'I take it that you don't approve?'

'Megan is entitled to live her own life. She seems to have a man for a year or so and then turns him in for another one. Usually she stays friends, though.'

'You disapprove of that?'

She was slightly irritated. 'It's not my business. It certainly isn't yours. I'll just say it wouldn't suit me.'

'No,' he said softly, 'I would have guessed that.' Delyth pressed the entry bell.

Megan was still in black. With a suppressed grin Delyth remembered her mother saying that a week with Megan was like staying in a funeral parlour. But, as ever, she looked striking. She was wearing a long velvet dress that caressed her figure, more opulent than

Delyth's. Her jewellery was silver again, a chain belt
and broad necklace with studs of jet. 'Good to see you
both,' she said. 'James, I'm glad you came.'

He offered her the parcel. 'I brought you a little
bread-and-butter present,' he said. 'I'm trying to ensure
that I get invited back.'

'I love surprises,' Megan squeaked. 'I'm going to
open it now.' She eased off the rich paper. Delyth, who
was just as intrigued, noticed the care with which it
had been wrapped. James's surgeon skills, no doubt.

Eventually Megan pulled off the last sheet of tissue
paper and the sisters looked at what was inside. It was
a carving in dark stone of— Was it a man's face?
Whatever it was, it was ugly, Delyth thought. She
looked at her sister and realised Megan was entranced.
'This is for me?' Megan asked, her voice low. 'It's
lovely but you can't give it away.'

'I can,' he said. 'It was given to me by someone
who valued it, and I'm pleased to give it to someone
else who will also value it. I don't like collecting
things—it's just been lying in a drawer.'

'It's beautiful. James, are you sure?'

'Certain. I don't want it. I suspect Delyth thinks it's
ugly—I could tell by what you were looking at this
morning that you'd like it.'

'I'm going to show it to people,' Megan announced.
'Come and meet a few.'

Megan's parties were always fun. Her mother had once
said that Megan collected friends with the same care
as most people picked furniture. There was a large living room, opening out onto an open balcony—just

enough space to let twenty-odd people eddy about,
talking and drinking. Delyth didn't stay with James all
the time. Everyone here was so friendly, she felt she
didn't need to. For a while she chatted to a man who
introduced himself as Charles Kay, a barrister who
lived in one of the other flats in the house. Then she
found herself refereeing an argument between two
friends, both in checked open-necked shirts, about the
relative merits of *Eastenders* and *Coronation Street.*
Then James fetched her to defend Wales as a holiday
destination rather than Scotland. It was that kind of
party.

She drank spritzers, and watched approvingly as
James drank beer sparingly. She noticed he was a suc-
cess at the party, being able to be pleasant without
being obtrusive. The more she saw of him, the more
she liked him. For a while, she thought, he was less
driven, more relaxed.

The party was still going strong when she walked
with Megan down to the front door to say goodbye to
one of the guests who had to leave early. His name
was Jennett, and he was a portrait painter.

'You should do a bronze of your sister,' he told
Megan. 'She has a glorious Celtic face.'

'Like to but I can't,' Megan said briefly. 'She's too
close to me. I couldn't distance myself.'

This made no sense to Delyth, but Jennett seemed
to understand. 'I see,' he said sadly. 'A pity, though.'

'I'm really enjoying myself,' Delyth said as she
climbed back up the stairs. 'And I think James—'

It had never happened so quickly before. A rush of
pain and horror. The sudden realisation was so unex-

pected that she had to hang onto the bannister, scared she might fall. It was like sharing someone's pain. She leaned there, white-faced, trying to grasp what had happened.

'Delyth! Are you all right?' Megan rushed back to her and eased her till she was sitting on the stairs, then put an arm round her. 'Are you feeling ill? Anything you've eaten or drunk?'

It wasn't that kind of pain. She shook her head. 'I just feel a bit faint. I'll be all right in a minute.'

Megan leaned her against the wall. 'What you need is a doctor. Good thing we've got one.' She ran to her flat door, ignoring Delyth's feeble protests. A minute later she reappeared with James.

He knelt in front of her. In spite of his obvious concern, he was the efficient doctor, taking her pulse and feeling her forehead. 'A bit erratic but nothing much to worry about,' he said after a while. 'What exactly happened, Delyth? Did you run up the stairs too quickly?'

It was nothing like that. And the knowledge hit her again. She wasn't in pain—it was someone else. 'Who lives in that flat?' she asked Megan, pointing to the door on the other side of the landing.

Megan looked puzzled. 'Why, it's Charles Kay— you were talking to him before. He left earlier—he's got an important case starting on Monday and needs to look through his brief. Why?'

'Someone in that flat is dangerously ill,' Delyth said. 'Dying even.'

Megan shook her head. 'Charles lives alone. And you saw him. He's in excellent health.'

'If he's alone then he's dying, I tell you.'

Now it was James's turn to be serious and concerned. 'Can you give us any good reason why you think that, Delyth?'

She couldn't. She knew they thought her foolish, and perhaps she was. Maybe she should just forget about it, rejoin the party and have another drink. And the minute she considered it, the certainty was there again, stronger than ever. Somebody needed help. 'We need to talk to him,' she persisted.

She didn't like the way James was looking at her, as if she were a hysterical girl. He was just being accommodating because she was being stupid. The thought irritated her. 'Can we at least ring his doorbell?' she said. 'He won't have gone to bed yet.'

'He won't like being disturbed,' Megan muttered. 'But if you have to...'

There was no answer to their ring, or to the second and third. 'I'll go in the flat and phone him,' Megan said. 'He may be in his study.'

James and Delyth stayed outside. Delyth kept her eyes fixed on the floor, but she couldn't remain silent and eventually she asked, 'You think I'm being stupid, don't you?'

His reply was calm, reasonable. 'I think you may be wrong, Delyth. But stupid is the last thing I would ever call you.'

His very reasonableness irritated her. 'We'll just have to wait and see, won't we?' she snapped. After that they both remained silent.

Megan reappeared. 'It's ringing but there's no reply,'

she said. 'And I'm certain he's in. D'you think he could be in the bath or something?'

'He's not in the bath,' Delyth said flatly.

Unhappily, Megan produced a key. 'We each have a key to the other's flat. In case of a flood or something. But I've never been in without an invitation. If we go barging in and he's working or something, then he's not going to be well pleased.'

It was James who answered. 'Ring for the last time. If there's no answer, we'll let ourselves in. If we look fools, then so be it.'

There was no reply to their ringing. James took the key and opened the door. 'Charles…are you there?' Megan called. There was still no answer. The three entered a hall with the light still on, and walked forward. The door was opened to one room, and they peered in. It was a study. Delyth caught a glimpse of an antique desk, book-lined walls. But on the floor was a figure, in shirt and trousers, with blood in a pool round the head.

As Megan cowered into the background, James and Delyth knelt at each side of Charles. James felt the neck and nodded at Delyth. 'He's breathing and he's got a pulse, weak and irregular but it's there. Can we take a look at that cut? Megan, there's a phone there. Ring 999 for an ambulance.'

Delyth sprang to her feet, found the kitchen and took a damp clean cloth. Carefully she wiped away the blood from the injured head. There was a clean cut there, long but not deep. She compressed the cloth over it.

'Head wounds bleed a lot,' James muttered, 'but I

doubt this is enough to cause unconsciousness. 'Breathing very shallow…'

She looked round. 'There's blood on the corner of the desk, James. He could have caught his head as he fell. But why did he—?'

They both guessed at once. 'Heart attack,' James said. 'He's still breathing but he could arrest at any minute. Megan, fetch a couple of pillows, will you? If we have him in a semi-recumbent position it will ease the strain on his heart.'

Megan did as requested, and Delyth and James eased Charles over and slid the pillows under his head and shoulders. Is…he going to be all right?' Megan asked.

'We need to get him to hospital where they have the proper equipment,' James said. 'The paramedics will have some of it. Otherwise, we just sit here and hope he doesn't arrest. If he does, then it's mouth-to-mouth and external heart massage.'

'I'll go down to meet the ambulance,' Megan said. 'Did you know there's still a party going on in my flat?'

James was unusually silent in the taxi going home. The party had broken up when the ambulance arrived. Megan had gone to hospital with Charles and would try to get in touch with his relations. Delyth couldn't work out James's mood. He seemed irritated, almost angry. She decided to say nothing.

'We've got a problem, Delyth,' he said when they finally stepped out of the taxi. 'I suspect you saved that man's life.'

'*We* saved his life,' she corrected him. 'And, if anything, the paramedics did most.' As ever, the green-coated figures had efficiently taken charge at once. 'Why, what's the problem?'

They stood facing each other in the quad, the lights of St Helen's all around them. When he didn't answer at once she said, 'The party finished in rather a hurry. Would you like to come to my room for a coffee and we can talk?'

'Yes,' he said, 'I would like that.'

He sat on her bed, took off his coat and loosened his tie. She went to switch on the percolator in the kitchen then changed from her blue dress into a track-suit in the bathroom. When they both were clutching mugs of coffee, she asked, 'What's the matter, James?'

He had obviously thought out what he was going to say. 'You're going to tell me that some mysterious sixth sense told you that Charles Kay was ill. You knew because you are the seventh child of a seventh child—or some such mumbo-jumbo.'

'I didn't say it was because I was a seventh child,' she protested. 'I told you that almost as a joke.' She felt like fighting back. 'Anyway, if it wasn't a sixth sense, how did I know?'

'Good point,' he conceded grudgingly, 'but still quite answerable. Like I said before, you're a trained doctor—you've learned more than you realise. When you talked to the man earlier you subconsciously recognised the signs of an incipient heart attack. I'm impressed. But it's got nothing to do with the supernatural. Just admit it, Delyth!'

She thought a while. 'You're angry again,' she said, 'and I don't know why. It's not just that I'm being unscientific, it's more than that. Please tell me what it is.'

There was a long pause, so long that she thought he wasn't going to answer. Then he said, 'I'm an orphan. My parents were in a car crash when I was two. When I was eighteen I felt I had to know what happened so I looked up what had happened. I checked in newspapers, hospital records, family papers. My father was killed at once. My mother was badly injured, but she survived.'

He drank from his mug. Delyth kept silent. When he spoke his voice was thick. 'In hospital my mother came under the influence of a faith healer. In spite of all good advice, she was persuaded to sign herself out of hospital. Three weeks later she was back in again, and she died the next day. Technical cause of death, pneumonia. Real cause of death, neglect. Instead of antibiotics, this self-styled healer had been burning leaves under her nose. She said she had divined the spiritual cause of the sickness. I looked her up. She died of drink eight years later.'

Delyth put her hand on his arm. 'I'm so sorry,' she said. 'My family means everything to me. I just can't imagine being without one.'

'Being without a family has its good points. It means no one has a call on you.'

It seemed a sad note on which to end a wonderful day.

CHAPTER THREE

On Sunday morning Delyth had the rarest of pleasures, an extra two hours in bed. She sat there, reading, feeling suitably decadent. Then Megan rang her.

'Charles is out of danger and very grateful. I've located his sister—she's coming down from the Midlands this afternoon. I must say, youngest sister, you make my parties more exciting than I really like.'

'Just luck we were there,' Delyth said cautiously.

'Good luck for Charles. I don't understand it. Do people have massive heart attacks without warning? I thought you usually had little ones first.'

'It can happen that way. But ischaemic heart disease kills a lot of people and it can strike anyone at almost any age. Charles will probably have to alter his lifestyle.'

Megan was dubious. 'Hmm. He won't like that.' She decided to change the subject. 'How serious are you about James? You've only just met him and yet you seem to be seeing a lot of him. I know you. You've never had much time for men before—why pick on this one?'

'I think he's special,' Delyth said simply.

'He's special all right. And that carving he gave me is wonderful—I don't know how he could bear to part with it. I like him, but I don't know if he's the one for you.'

'Something about his face?' Delyth asked sardoni-
cally. 'Something you can see that I can't?'

'Perhaps I'm wrong. I hope so. Keep in touch.'
Megan rang off.

In her dressing-gown Delyth padded down the corridor to make herself some tea, then sat in bed again
and thought. Unusually for her, she hadn't thought
much about herself and James. She had been content
to let things develop as they would. She realised she
had felt a blithe confidence that everything would be
all right. Compared with the agonising she had gone
through with previous boyfriends, that was amazing.

She wasn't stupid. She knew she was attractive to
men. She liked the company of men—got on well with
Matt, for example. While training she had had a number of boyfriends, but there had never been one whom
she'd thought could have been the only man for her.
She had liked them, felt comfortable with them, even
admired a couple. But she'd never felt she could really
love any of them. With a shock, she realised that James
could be different. She had felt the attraction the first
time they'd met. Since then every meeting had made
her more and more certain.

Why was that such an unsettling thought? She didn't
really know how he felt about her. Certainly he liked
her, but did he feel the same about her as she felt about
him? Just for a moment she had some idea of what
people meant when they said that love hurt. It had
never hurt in the past. The worst she had felt when
parting from someone had been a mild regret. But with
James her life was going to change.

It would be polite to let him know how Charles was.

She knew he was on the ward so she phoned and left a non-urgent message that Charles was all right. An hour later he phoned back—as she had secretly hoped he would.

'I'm pleased about Charles,' he said, 'and I enjoyed the party and meeting Megan. Are there really another five like you two?'

'I'm afraid so. And my mother as well. You must meet them all some time.'

'I'd like that— Oh, excuse me a minute.' Delyth could hear the rumble of conversation. Someone had thought something important enough to interrupt him.

'Sorry about that,' he said when he came back. 'We're busy here. Look, I've got a meeting at another hospital tonight, but can we have another late drink in the Clubroom tomorrow night? Say the last half-hour?'

She thought rapidly. 'Love to, but it'll have to be late. I'm going to listen to some jazz again. I wouldn't normally, but I used to know the band from home.'

'From home? A Welsh jazz band?' His voice was comically disbelieving.

'The Welsh are a musical race,' she said, mock-primly. 'All sorts of music, too.'

'I believe you. If you're seeing friends, would you like to put our drink off till another night?'

'No. I'd much rather have a drink with you,' she said. Then she sat, appalled at her own honesty.

'Half ten tomorrow night, then.' Behind him, she could hear the sound of another voice. 'Must go, Delyth.'

I hope he doesn't think I'm one of those young doctors who throws herself at the senior staff, she thought as she replaced the receiver. Then she decided that she was certain that he didn't.

'Birdie Jones is talking about signing himself out,' an anxious young junior nurse told Delyth next morning. 'Says he's fed up with lying still in hospital and wants to get out again.'

Delyth looked up from the pile of reports she was filling in, and frowned. This was a not unusual problem. Patients had the right, of course, to take themselves out of hospital at any time that suited them. Most accepted the doctors' advice as to the best time to leave, but some—particularly drug addicts—just had to get back on the streets. Usually they came back a few weeks later in a much worse state. But she didn't think Birdie was a junkie. 'Any special reason he wants to leave?' she asked.

'He says he's got things to do. But he won't say what.'

'I'll come and have a word with him,' Delyth decided. 'He's just not capable of living on his own at present.'

But Birdie thought otherwise. 'You can't keep me here if I don't want to stay,' he said belligerently. 'I'll come to have my dressings changed in the clinic. You can have the bed for some poor devil who needs it.'

'You're the poor devil who needs it,' she told him. 'Birdie, don't you realise how close you were to dying? And you're still very weak. You need the hospital rest.'

She saw the sudden flash of fear cross his face, quickly replaced by his usual impassive stare. 'I've got my own reasons for wanting to get out,' he said.

It was the first indication he'd given that there was some special reason for his wish to leave. Delyth seized her advantage. 'Come on, tell me. It's not your family, is it? You said you'd lost touch with them.'

'I have. But it's sort of family.' Birdie, the streetwise hard man, looked embarrassed. 'It's my dog. He's called Reginald.'

'Reginald?' asked Delyth, managing to keep a straight face.

'I had to call him something. Anyway, we usually sleep in that underpass near Marble Arch. He won't mind too much if I'm missing for a while and he'll hang around there for a day or two, and one or two of me mates will give him the odd scrap. But if I'm gone for long he might leave for good.'

'There's nowhere he can stay in the hospital,' she said.

'I know. That's why I've got to get out.'

'You'll kill yourself. Just lie there and let me think a bit. There must be some kind of solution.' This is a funny kind of a medical problem, she thought.

Half an hour later she thought she perhaps had a solution. She went back to Birdic's bedside. 'How often does Reginald get fed?' she asked.

Birdie shrugged. 'He gets half of what I get. But it's not much of a feast usually.'

'I know dogs. Would he stay near the underpass if he was fed regularly?'

'Wouldn't he just? But how—?'

'If I gave him some money, would one of your mates feed the dog every day?'

'Andy would. But I haven't got—'

'I'll lend you some money. I'll take it to Andy and he can buy stuff for Reginald. Can I trust Andy with the money?'

'If it's for the dog, 'course you can,' Birdie said indignantly. 'He's got a dog of his own, he knows what it's like. But why should you lend me money? I'm just a rough sleeper, a beggar.'

She shrugged. 'It's for your dog. I think you'll pay me back.'

He looked at her in silence. 'I will,' he said. 'It might take time but I will.'

In her lunchbreak Delyth took a taxi to Marble Arch and walked into the complex of tunnels underneath. Andy was sitting on the floor where Birdie had said he'd be, a bearded, long-haired figure in an ex-army greatcoat, his arm round an equally scruffy dog. A surprisingly intelligent eye looked at her when she asked his name.

She explained who she was, where Birdie was and how worried he was about Reginald. Then she offered the figure three five-pound notes. 'Ten pounds for dog food,' she said, 'and a further five pounds for yourself.'

Andy took ten pounds and offered her five back. In a cultured voice he said, 'Thank you for looking after Birdie and bothering to come down here. I'll happily take the money for Reginald. But on this occasion there's no need to give me anything.'

She pushed the note back to him. 'Then buy something for your dog. Bye, Andy.'

She caught a taxi back to work. The entire trip had

taken only twenty minutes, and when she reported to Birdie he looked much happier.

Many people in hospital, she knew, would think that she'd acted foolishly. Her job was to treat people for illnesses, not act as a social worker. But she felt good.

Then, as she left Birdie's little side-ward, a nurse said, 'Could you have a word with Mrs Webster? She's had nothing to eat today. She's a bit…upset.'

The oncology registrar had been to see Mrs Webster. The results of the mammogram and fine needle biopsy had only confirmed what everyone had already guessed—the lump was malignant. Now Mrs Webster was scheduled for a lumpectomy and then radiotherapy.

Giving news like this, it was always difficult. The registrar had explained things as carefully as possible, and had made himself available for further explanations when Mr Webster came in to visit that evening. At first it seemed that Wendy had accepted her bad news with resignation, but it now turned out that the resignation had been incomprehension. She just could not come to terms with having cancer.

When Delyth entered her little room Wendy raised a tear-blotched face from her pillow. 'What d'you want?' she asked. 'Not more examinations. I've had enough.'

Delyth was getting used to aggression. It wasn't an uncommon reaction to bad news. Sitting on the bed, she said gently, 'I've just come to see if you're all right, Wendy. Why haven't you eaten anything today?'

'What's the point of eating if I'm going to die anyway? I only came in here to have my legs done. If I'd known this was going to happen I wouldn't have come.'

'Nobody says you're going to die,' Delyth said carefully. 'Certainly, you're more ill than you thought, but we've caught things early. I should be optimistic if I were you.'

'You're not me! You're not married. What'll Harry do if I die?'

'There's no need to talk of dying. Now, you need to keep your strength up. Can I get you a sandwich or something?'

'I thought you said I was overweight. Why are you trying to feed me?'

And so it went on. Delyth knew that Wendy was incapable of reasonable argument. Her fear was beyond logic. For a while she considered prescribing a beta-blocker, a pill to lower anxiety, but decided against it. Eventually, perhaps soothed by the constant reassurance, Wendy grew calmer. 'I'll get a nurse to fetch you something to eat,' Delyth said, making her escape. 'You'll feel better then.'

She felt drained by the short interview. Medicine isn't just drugs, she told herself.

By evening she was looking forward to her evening of listening to jazz. She arrived early at the pub and asked to go to the tiny room where the band was unpacking. She knew they'd be busy. For an amateur group there was often more work backstage than on-stage. Their leader, Alex Llewellyn, was pleased to meet an old friend, as were the others. At one stage she had seen a lot of the band, but inevitably their paths had divided.

'Where's Meriel?' she asked, referring to the band's singer.

'She's left us. Earning large sums of money, doing something with computers. Now we're working we don't get together as often as we used to.' It was the usual fate of student bands, even the good ones. 'Going to stay behind for a bit of a party afterwards?' Alex asked.

'Can't,' she said. 'Tomorrow I must work.' It had been fun, being a student.

When the band went on stage she sat with Matt and the others, who were regular attendees at the live jazz nights. Matt offered her a drink. She asked for ginger beer and ice.

'Heard you went out with James Owen on Saturday night,' he said, elaborately casually.

'I took him to a party at my sister's.' There was no keeping anything quiet in a hospital. Not that she particularly wanted to keep her relationship quiet. And James didn't seem to mind.

'Lucky James,' Matt said, but she thought he didn't mean it unpleasantly.

They listened to the band play. This wasn't a traditional band like the one which had played last time. It was quieter, with a line-up of bass, drums, keyboard and guitar. But they were skilful musicians, and she enjoyed the playing. Matt and his pals weren't quite so keen, although they listened and applauded politely. In the intervals between the numbers they talked about football. Delyth winced.

'I asked,' a voice said. 'Ginger beer and ice. I'm even going to try one myself.'

She looked up. There was James, two drinks in his hands. It was just because it was unexpected, that was all, but her heart gave a mighty thump, she felt her mouth go dry and she couldn't at once reply.

Casual again, he was dressed in jeans and a light blue T-shirt. The lights were lowered in the pub, but the power of her eyesight seemed more intense. She could see the wisps of hair on his forearms. She noticed the way the T-shirt creased as it tucked into the flat waist of his jeans, even the mobile phone attached to his belt.

She thought she must look foolish, sitting there unable to speak, mouth half-open. It was less than forty-eight hours since she had last seen him yet she was struck dumb by him. He was growing on her; the face she'd thought not really handsome now had a tremendous attraction. He smiled. 'Room for a little one?'

She slid sideways to let him in. He sat, and nodded to the others, telling them that he'd enjoyed it so much last time that he couldn't keep away. They smiled and nodded back, but Delyth saw the sudden sharp glance Matt directed at her.

She managed to speak. 'I'm not supposed to see you till half past ten,' she said, and instantly felt annoyed with her clumsy remark. She was twenty-four years old, a doctor, and she was still acting like a young teenager on her first date.

'Sorry,' he said urbanely, 'but I got fed up with work and I remembered how much I enjoyed myself here last time. You don't mind me coming, do you?'

'Of course not! It's open to anyone, isn't it? I didn't mean that. We're pleased to see you and...'

He laid his hand on her arm, and his touch thrilled her. Laughing, he said, 'I'm very glad to be here. Now let's listen.'

Fortunately the band struck up again. She needed a few minutes to calm herself. Alex and his friends were playing a clever arrangement of 'Sweet Georgia Brown', and she enjoyed the jazz classic. When they'd finished she clapped with the others, having regained her composure. 'I *am* glad you've come,' she said more calmly. 'You should enjoy Alex's music.'

'I came to be with you,' he replied. 'The music is just an extra.' And she felt flustered again. 'Are we still having that last drink in the Clubhouse?' he went on.

She didn't hesitate. 'Yes,' she said firmly. 'I'm looking forward to it.'

After that the conversation became more general, James taking part in a heated argument about medical politics. Should there be a vast increase in the number of consultants? Delyth noticed with some amusement that Matt and the other two were conservatives, saying that the numbers were about right, and James was arguing for expansion. As ever, James argued vehemently but not overbearingly. Delyth was almost sorry when the band started again.

She was enjoying herself. There were five of them on the banquette, now pushed together. She was aware of the warmth of James, the feeling of his bare arm against hers, the length of his muscled thigh pressing through the thinness of her skirt. It was…exciting.

The band finished to more enthusiastic applause. Alex thanked everybody, said how much they liked playing here and how they were always made welcome. 'A lot of people have asked about Meriel, our singer,' he went on. 'Well, sadly, she's now making her fortune in computers. But there's someone here who's sung with us in the past and we'd like to ask her to join us now for just one song before the interval. Delyth Price!'

For the second time that evening Delyth was shocked. She shouldn't have been—this had happened before. She didn't stand at once, and a grinning band member swung a spotlight on her. People turned to look.

Beside her James was bemused. 'You can sing?' he muttered.

Led by the band, the applause grew louder. 'Oh, I can sing all right,' she whispered, and stood to walk to the band. She wasn't nervous. She knew she could sing in public.

'You might have warned me,' she grumbled to Alex as she climbed onto the dais.

He smiled. 'You should sing more than you do. And lots of people asked for Meriel and I knew you were just as good. What can you remember?'

She had already decided. 'I want to sing "Summertime".'

'That's great. Let's go.'

She was confident in the introduction and knew she'd fit in well with the band. She'd sung this with them before. Unconsciously she clasped her hands, the way she always did when singing, waited for her moment and started on the long, drawn-out first notes. It wasn't an easy song, but it was an effective one. She was happy in the spotlight, for a moment in the career she could have taken up instead of medicine.

When she finished the applause was louder than it had been all evening, and there were calls for an encore, but Alex wouldn't put on her. The house lights came up and he said firmly they would be back after the interval. Delyth walked back to rejoin her friends, smiling at people who clapped her as she passed. She had forgotten the buzz she used to get from performing. Now she was rather smugly aware of the shock she had caused James, Matt and his friends.

James was smiling but silent, the others rather boisterous in their congratulations. When she sat by him he whispered, 'Delyth, that was wonderful. How many more ways are you going to amaze me?'

'There's a lot to me you don't know,' she said cheerfully. 'I used to sing an awful lot.' Now thoroughly confident, she looked at her watch. 'It's a quarter past ten. D'you still want to go to the Clubhouse?'

He looked startled. 'Yes. But don't you want to stay longer?'

'I decided earlier that I'd leave now. Shall we go?'

They left, James somehow making it obvious to the others that they weren't invited. Delyth saw Matt looking glum, and hoped she wasn't going to have trouble with him. She did quite like him.

By now she was used to James's rapid pace through the streets. He was silent as they first walked so she commented, 'You're quiet.'

'I was thinking of your singing. Why didn't you tell me you had such a glorious voice?'

She felt happy at the compliment. 'It never came up,'

she pointed out. 'I can't just say out of the blue, "I've got a glorious voice." And it doesn't have much to do with medicine.'

'You're good enough to be a professional,' he said abruptly. 'Did you never think of it?'

'Just a bit. My family were very keen—they're all something artistic except me. I'm the unusual one. My sisters think I'm odd. But I always knew that I was going to be a doctor. I didn't even worry that I wouldn't get the grades—I just knew I would.'

'Hmm. I'm only just realising how little I know about you.'

'How could you?' she asked. 'We only met five days ago.'

He looked startled. 'Good Lord, you're right. But it feels...like ages.' He took her hand, and she squeezed his. 'This isn't like me,' he said.

'I know. Everyone I've talked to in hospital is a little bit frightened of you. They say you're a very good doctor but you're driven—you don't like mistakes. They hate it when you frown at them.'

'Thank you for that comprehensive character assassination,' he said drily. 'Are you afraid of me, Delyth?'

They had just reached the Saracen's Head. She entered and walked down the passage to the Clubroom like a regular. His question was an interesting one, she realised. 'No, I'm not afraid of you,' she said slowly. 'And I know I ought to be. I was terrified when I was in my last year of training and the prof. told me off. Even though he did it like a gentleman. Usually I'm very much in awe of those in authority. Why don't you frighten me?'

'I must be slipping,' he told her. 'I used to terrify young house officers.'

They entered the Clubroom; she recognised quite a few people there. In a corner there was a group of slightly older nurses, obviously celebrating a birthday or something, who were getting rather noisily drunk. They waved to James, and he waved back cheerfully. 'Come and join us!' a nurse of about forty with a rather hard face shouted.

James shook his head. 'We're not here to enjoy ourselves. Delyth and I have business to talk over.'

The rest of the group seemed happy with this, but the nurse who had called looked sour. 'Suit yourself,' she said.

'You're a quick liar,' Delyth whispered to him as they sat down. 'You just didn't want to go over there, did you?'

'Nothing worse than being sober when all around you aren't. We'll sit here quietly and I'll fetch us more ginger beer.' He left her to go to the hatch, and just for a moment she was aware of the malevolent stare of the hard-faced nurse. Why?

They sipped their chilled soft drinks. There was something she felt she had to tell him. 'You were asking why I don't feel frightened of you. And I can see that you're a frightening man. For some reason I feel all right with you. And, James, I'm not usually a forward young woman. It's just that I—'

'Don't say that you've got powers,' he said with a grin. 'You just feel the same about me as I feel about you. We're attracted. It's lovely, and I feel the world is a better place because of it, but basically it's pheromones. Simple animal attraction.'

She dug him viciously in the ribs with her finger. 'Don't treat me as a chemistry set. There's more to me than that. It's just that something is telling me that I'm...all right with you. I've never felt it with any other man either.'

He looked at her thoughtfully. 'You really mean that, don't you? Delyth, I'm a scientist like you, a rationalist. I don't like mystical ideas.'

'I do mean it,' she said helplessly. 'James, I know these ideas aren't scientific. I've tried to get rid of them, but they're part of me.'

He put his arm round her waist. 'I still like you a lot,' he said. Somehow, that made things seem better.

The group across the room stood and noisily started to leave, the hard-faced nurse waving again. James smiled at her, but Delyth felt there was something threatening in the smile. She felt a bit sorry for the nurse. 'Have you ever drunk too much?' she asked. 'I mean, ever found yourself drinking because you had to?'

He frowned. She didn't know why she had asked. She'd expected him to say no at once. But he paused before answering. 'There was a time when it was a definite temptation. When things get on top of you it's very easy to have a quick Scotch, and another... Then you find yourself looking forward to getting home so you can have the first.'

She was amazed at this. James always seemed so much in control. 'You didn't really have a problem?' she asked.

He laughed. 'No. Just once I got close enough to realise there could be a problem if I let it.'

The hard-faced nurse put her head round the door and shouted, 'We're off now. Evening, all.' She looked directly at James. ''Night, Angel.' Then she was dragged off by her friends.

The two sat in silence for a moment. Then Delyth said, 'You don't usually let your emotions show, do you? You've got a stone face—or you can have. But just for a moment there I could see you were hurt when she called you ''Angel''. Why?' She thought, then said, 'You don't have to tell me if you don't want to.'

She wondered if she had gone too far. He remained silent, his face impassive. Then he said absently, 'That was Staff Nurse Bentley. I've known her vaguely for years. She'll be sorry she said that when she sobers.'

'If she remembers,' Delyth said sharply. 'She meant it to hurt.'

'True.' He emptied his glass and set it smartly back on the table with a rap. 'Just for a minute there I was tempted to fetch myself a whisky. Silly idea. I'm on call.'

There was another pause, then he went on, 'You would have heard about this in time, Delyth. You can't hide anything in hospital. I did intend to tell you. It's something perhaps you should know. She called me Angel—it's short for Angel of Death.'

'That's not very nice,' Delyth said, 'for a doctor.'

He went on emotionlessly. 'I was engaged to be married once—to another doctor. We trained together, her name was Erin Shaw. We'd been together since we were eighteen and we wanted to stay together. I loved her.'

Delyth tried to ignore the ignoble shaft of jealousy that twisted inside her. 'Go on,' she said. 'What happened?'

'She died. We were both working very hard—house doctors, like you now. She didn't pay enough attention to herself, thought she was just tired. It's a joke, isn't it, training to be a doctor, spotting other people's illnesses and ignoring your own? She thought she was just run down, but she had leukaemia. It took three months from illness to death.'

Delyth was shocked at the sheer horror of the story, at the matter-of-fact way he told it. But then she looked at his teak face, and knew that he was feeling it all again. 'When was this?' she asked.

'A long time ago now, over eight years.'

She was going to say something which she knew would be trite, something about how time would heal everything. They she looked at him more closely and asked, 'There's something else, isn't there?'

'Afraid so. It took me time to get over Erin's death. I did it largely by working like a lunatic. But in time I did get over it. And after a while I found another girl, Hilary Tennyson. Not a doctor, a nurse this time. She helped me get over Erin's death—she'd known her, had nursed her. I began to enjoy life again and, in fact, we were living together. Then she was hit by a runaway lorry and never recovered consciousness. Died after three days.'

He turned to her with a savage smile. 'Going out with me could be dangerous, Delyth. Women I love seem to die. One of the nurses called me the Angel of Death. The nickname stuck.'

There was nothing Delyth could say. She stared at him, white-faced.

CHAPTER FOUR

BEING a house officer might seem never-ending, but it was always interesting. Delyth knew she was learning. Although she could always ask for advice, she had a lot to decide herself. After her two days off she had a run in which she seemed to be working more time than there was in a week. Her hours were supposed to be limited, but if the work was there it had to be done.

Frank Allison looked at her suspiciously. He was seventy, and had never come across anything like this in his life. 'It can't be natural,' he said, 'putting machines inside people and leaving them there. And you say it'll be powered by a battery? All the batteries I've ever had have run out after a month. I'm not being cut open every month.'

'These are special, very expensive batteries,' she told him. 'They last about ten years. And if you have a pacemaker fitted you'll feel a lot better. You won't be so tired and there'll be a lot less discomfort.'

'Why didn't you fit one when I came in, then? Without telling me?'

'We need to have your consent, Frank. We can't just operate on you. You have to decide whether you want the operation or not.'

Frank considered this. 'Are you absolutely certain that nothing can go wrong?'

This was a difficult question to answer, but she had

been told to be absolutely honest. 'There's a risk to everything, Frank. But we can say that about one in every two thousand people has been fitted with one. And they all feel the benefit.'

'So, what exactly will you do?'

'You have it done under local anaesthetic. No need for sending you to sleep. But we'll probably give you something to relax you. And it'll take no longer than an hour. Afterwards you carry a card round to say you've been fitted with a pace maker, and some people wear a bracelet with the details on.'

'I'm not wearing a bracelet! You'll be fitting me with earrings next!'

Delyth knew the old man was being awkward on purpose, obviously enjoying the conversation.

'I think you'd look sweet in earrings,' she said. 'But they're not necessary and the bracelet's not compulsory. Now, what they do is fix a little wire in your heart and attach it to this tiny machine which we put inside your chest. You might be able to feel it if you touch it. But what you certainly will be able to feel is a lot better.'

'Not tired all the time?'

Once again she had to be careful. 'Almost certainly you'll feel a lot better. But I'd be wrong if I didn't tell you that there's a tiny risk.'

'All right,' said Frank, 'where d'you want me to sign?'

Delyth took out the form for him. Before an operation all patients had to give their informed consent. 'Informed' was the important word. It was no good just saying that an operation was necessary. The patient had to be informed of any risks, and have a clear idea of what was involved.

Occasionally she saw James on the ward, always moving with his customary speed. He would smile at her as if they shared a secret, and she would smile back. He phoned her and said, 'I know you have no time for eating or sleeping, much less washing, but how about a stolen half-hour in the Clubroom?'

After that they got into the habit of meeting there as often as they could. He had to take a series of clinics in a neighbouring smaller hospital so often he didn't get back till late. He would phone, and they would snatch a few minutes together. Togetherness was all she needed, all she had time for, all she could cope with.

Their short meetings were odd. Both seemed to know that something might develop, but neither was sure what. For the moment they were busy—things would take their time.

Then, after a fortnight's hard but exciting work, she found herself with two whole days off. 'It's midweek,' she announced to him as they sat in the Clubroom, 'Wednesday and Thursday. But days are days.'

'What are you going to do? See Megan again? A bit more of London?'

'Sleep,' she said with some passion. 'Then wash my clothes, clean my room, write letters to family and friends. I might even do a little light reading.'

'All excellent ideas.' They were sitting together in the rather distant corner that had become particularly theirs. No one could overhear their conversation; people didn't come to sit with them unless invited.

'You could do all those on Wednesday,' he continued. 'How long since you had any fresh air?'

'They don't make it around here. I'm getting quite fond of diesel fumes and carbon monoxide.'

'Just as I thought. Look, I can take Thursday afternoon off. The forecast isn't bad—how about seeing the best London can do for countryside? Get out your boots and trousers and I'll pick you up at one.' He looked at her, suddenly thoughtful. 'You do walk, don't you?'

'I'm a country girl. Of course I do.'

'Good. And just for once we'll have a rule. No talk of medicine.'

'Is that possible?' she asked demurely.

'Quite possible. In fact, we'll have no depressing talk at all.'

That was a coded message she recognised. He didn't want to talk about his past. When he'd told her about his two dead lovers a fortnight before, she had been too upset to ask for details. She remembered his account of the deaths of his parents—what a load for any man to bear! After he had told her he had taken her back to the residence and kissed her gently. She had grabbed him and pulled him to her, her face next to his. She had wanted to give him comfort and she thought he had recognised this.

After a while he had put her from him, equally gently. 'I'm all right really,' he had said. 'We'll talk about it some time—if you want to, that is.'

'If you want to tell me,' she had answered. But since

then there just hadn't been time.

I'd really like a walk,' she told him.

Delyth still hadn't seen much of the centre of London, and the outskirts were completely new to her. James took her by train from Waterloo to Kingston-on-Thames, and they walked across the river, and along the path by its side and on to Hampton Court Palace. Feeling like tourists, they wandered round, talking about history and admiring the ancient buildings. But James didn't intend to saunter for long. He'd brought her here to walk.

They walked back through Kingston and into Richmond Park. It took her a while, but she managed to get used to his long, loping pace. 'I'm certainly getting my exercise with you,' she panted.

'It's good for you. If more people walked further there'd be less work for us in hospital.'

'No talking shop,' she warned him.

It was good to feel the grass underfoot in the park. She saw the deer and almost felt she was in the country. But in the distance she could see the great towers of the city. He made her walk hard so her legs ached, her lungs stretched. Then they dropped down into Richmond and had a welcome cup of tea, sitting overlooking the river.

'I really enjoyed that,' she said. 'It was just what I needed. I know what you're doing—you're taking me out of myself, reminding me there is a life outside medicine.'

He reached over the table to squeeze her hand. 'You need to remember that,' he said seriously. 'It took me a long time to realise it. Learn from my mistakes.'

'I don't think of you making mistakes.'

'Everyone makes mistakes,' he told her soberly. 'Come on, we'll get the train back.'

It was rather fun to be on the train—there weren't too many on it. Most people were commuting back after a day in the City, and watching the crammed trains coming the other way gave her a sense of escape. 'I'm quite happily tired,' she told him as their train slid into the station. 'This has done me no end of good. But I hope our day isn't over yet.'

'Certainly not. I can either take you out to dinner or, if you want, you can come to my flat and I'll feed you there.'

'You're going to cook for me?'

'My domestic staff will knock something up,' he said urbanely. 'Now, which do you want to do?'

It seemed to be a casual invitation, but she knew it wasn't. When she accepted she had the sense of making a definite decision, of taking a step into something new. But she accepted anyway. Sometimes you had to take risks.

'I'll come to your flat,' she said, 'but I want to shower and change first. It'll take me about an hour.'

'Then shall I pick you up about seven?'

She shook her head. 'I wouldn't dream of it. You're close to the hospital and there are things you need to do. I'll be knocking on your door.'

'But I'd rather—'

'Just for once let me decide. You know it makes sense. You can walk me back if you like.'

He frowned, but he agreed.

For the walk she'd had her hair in her customary

French plait. Now she took it down and rinsed it through in the shower. She'd leave it long, caught back with pretty slides. She put on pretty, frilly underwear, again in white silk, then a grey dress, cool and attractive. No tights—it was too warm. Just a touch of make-up. She seemed to be acting without conscious volition. What the evening would bring she wasn't going to think about.

His flat was in a house owned by the hospital, only five minutes away and practically part of the complex. Three doctors each had a flat there. She was wondering as she rang the bell, but a kind of faith told her that everything would be all right.

He answered, dressed in dark trousers and a white shirt, his hair still wet. As ever, he looked wonderful. And she knew that, as he looked at her, he found her attractive too. His eyes burned with…admiration? When she saw him, all her previous tiny doubts disappeared. She was glad she had come.

'Delyth, come in.' He waved her through the door. 'I hope you're hungry. We'll dine in about half an hour. We'll have a drink first.'

She'd not been to his flat before. He escorted her to a living room, pleasant enough, with cream walls and a darkish carpet. When she sat on the couch he fetched two glasses and opened a bottle of wine. She liked the taste and the bubbles. Then he sat beside her. She looked round and frowned.

There was a television, a small CD player, a rack of books. Most of the books were medical tomes, dark and heavy. 'I recognise the furniture, curtains and paint,' she told him. 'They're all hospital issue.'

He shrugged. 'I just live here. Africa was even more basic than this, and I liked that, too. It suits me—most of my time here I spend working.'

'But there's nothing of you in the room! No pictures, no photographs.'

He seemed surprised at her protestation. 'What do I want pictures of, Delyth? You don't need pictures to bring back memories. I like to travel light. If I were offered a job in America I could be ready to leave tomorrow morning. I haven't even got a car.'

She shook her head in bewilderment. 'Is it all like this? May I look round?'

'It's all like this. But look round, anyway.'

Her mother had always said that a home told you everything about a person's character. But this flat told her nothing about James. Perhaps that was the point.

There was a bedroom with lowered Venetian blinds, throwing slats of light over the double bed. There was a spare room, neatly piled with cases. A dining annexe laid for two. Everything was scrupulously neat, but it said nothing about the inhabitant. The flat was as bland as a hotel room.

'I don't understand you,' she said. 'You're an interesting man, an interested man. But you've got nothing. Not even books.'

'Books I can get out of the library. I don't want roots, Delyth, things to cling to me. In the end you don't own possessions—they own you.'

'Perhaps,' she muttered, 'but they show who and what you are. All this…this nothingness. It's as if you're hiding yourself.'

He didn't answer her.

The kitchen looked as if it might be used sometimes, but that was all. The oven was on, and she stooped to peer through the glass door suspiciously. 'I'm ravenous, James. What about the meal I was promised? There's nothing in the oven. You're supposed to put food in it—it doesn't grow there.'

'Ah. I'd forgotten you were a country girl. I'll bet you are an expert cook.'

'My father has a market garden,' she said shortly. 'He grows a lot of our fresh food.'

The doorbell rang. 'Just in time,' he said cheerfully. 'I've no kitchen skills but I can certainly use a telephone.' He disappeared to open the door and returned followed by a little man, carrying a big tray. Quickly, the man stuffed foil-covered parcels into the oven or the fridge, and then disappeared.

'My good friend, Mr Hung,' said James. 'Shall we dine?'

'This is cheating,' she reproached him as they sat in the little annexe.

'Not at all. Mr Hung cooks wonderfully, I don't. On the other hand, I'm brilliant at taking out appendixes. A fair division of labour, I think. What d'you think of the menu we decided on together?'

She picked up the neatly written card Mr Hung had left on the table, and decided that this was a little more adventurous than the usual Chinese take-away. Melon with citrus fruits and blackcurrent sorbet. Cajun chicken with pepper sauce and a salad. A selection of ice creams and fresh raspberries and strawberries. 'Let's eat,' she said.

'That was a wonderful meal,' she sighed some time later. 'And I love the wine.'

He had opened another bottle—the first had seemed just to go. He had put on music, something low and seemingly distant. She recognised love songs from the Auvergne. They had decided not to bother with coffee as they still had wine. Now they sat side by side on the couch, pleasantly relaxed. He put his arm round her, and it seemed natural to rest her head against his chest and shoulder.

'I've had a good day,' she went on. 'I love being a doctor, but it's hard work. So when we have a rest from it I like to do something special. And today has been special.'

'It still is special,' he told her.

She turned and reached up to kiss his cheek. He hugged her tightly. 'I've enjoyed myself too,' he said. 'There's nobody I'd rather spend time with.'

She thought that they had all the time in the world. It was good just to be with him. She knew what would happen next and felt a tiny burst of apprehension. But there was no hurry.

After a while the arm round her shoulder tightened. He pulled her closer, leaned over and kissed her. He was gentle. She was conscious of him through all her senses, as if they were sharper, sensitised. There was the whisper of the rasp of his chin on her cheek. Through his thin white shirt she could feel his warmth, the muscles taut underneath. There was the rapid throb of a heart—whether his or hers she didn't know. She caught the faint musky scent of his expensive cologne. And how he kissed her!

Soft, feather-like kisses down the side of her face, almost tickling her on her ears. Then on her lips, still soft at first, but then more demanding, more passionate. She moaned softly as his mouth took hers, his tongue probing so she opened to him. His hand grazed her breast, more bold than ever before she took his hand and pressed it there. She heard his groan of excitement and then he slipped his hand inside her dress, to cup and caress her.

For a while it was heaven. Then he gasped. Sitting side by side, it was awkward, uncomfortable. 'Come and lie down with me,' he said.

There was a moment's hesitation, a sense of taking a step from which there would be no withdrawing. 'Yes,' she said simply.

He stood and drew her upright, pulled her against him so she could feel the movement of his chest as he breathed, the undoubted feeling of his masculinity. 'Are you sure?' he managed to ask.

She tugged his sleeve, turned to the bedroom. 'Of course I'm sure.' She smiled. 'Come on, I'm a big girl now.'

It was nearly dusk, the last rays of the sun tracing golden lines on the bed. He held her at arm's length; his face was serious but she could see the light of desire in his eyes. She wondered if her own face showed what she, too, was thinking.

She wouldn't merely be passive. This wasn't something that he was doing to her but something that they were doing together. Reaching forward, she unbuttoned his shirt and pulled it from his shoulders so she could see his lean body. Then he caught her to him and she thrilled to the rub of his naked flesh under her fingers.

Behind her, she felt his hands at her zip. He drew it slowly down and then tugged it over her shoulders so it fell in a soft grey froth at her feet. Now she was naked but for her shoes and the new bra and briefs, put on—specially for him? She wondered.

Kicking off her shoes was automatic, but she did nothing more. She knew he would want to undress her. His hands reached behind her, undid the clip of her bra, eased the scrap of silk forward. As he did so his hands touched the sides of her breasts, his fingertips exciting the pinkness of the erect tips. She sighed, closed her eyes. Now his hands were on her hips, and there was an odd feeling of freedom as he slipped down her briefs. She was nervous—but happy.

She gave a little gasp of shock as he grabbed her by thighs and shoulders, swung her into the air and laid her softly onto the bed. Sensually, she stretched, linked her hands behind her head and closed her eyes. She was defenceless, offering herself to him, and it made her so happy. She heard the hiss of his breath as he gazed down at her. 'Delyth, you're beautiful,' he groaned.

There was the rustle of clothes and he was beside her, also naked. For a while he just held her, and slowly the apprehension she was feeling died away.

He kissed her more freely now she was naked. She sighed and writhed at the feeling of his lips on the side of her throat, the touch of his tongue on her nipples, now hard with desire. His hands stroked the curve of her shoulders, the delicate flatness of her stomach, the roundness of her hips.

She felt passion flowing like liquid fire through her entire body, knew that it was readying itself for that which she so intensely desired. Still with her eyes closed, she reached up to him, ran her fingertips along the leanness of his body, felt the roughness of hair, the smoothness of skin, and then heard his sudden sob of excitement as she took his hardness into her hand for a moment.

Her arms wrapped themselves round his neck, pulled him across her, down to her. Almost of their own volition her legs spread apart. She felt an infinity of excitement, of apprehension, as his body gently came down to touch hers. 'I've wanted this so much,' he muttered thickly, 'Delyth, do you know how much I've wanted you?'

'I've wanted you too,' she reproved him. 'Surely you know that? I've kept myself for you, James. Something told me this was meant to be. I know we're destined to be together for ever. It'll always be like this.'

Her happiness lasted another thirty seconds. He was poised above her. She couldn't wait any longer so she urged him down towards her, into her. 'James,' she panted.

But there was something wrong. His body, which had been so ready, now seemed rigid with some kind of torment. He slumped to one side of her.

She opened her eyes and looked at the face next to her, now crushed into the bedding. 'James, what is it?' she asked tremulously.

His voice was now thick with some emotion other than passion. 'You said you know this is meant to be.'

'Yes…I know it. Surely you feel it, too?'

He didn't answer her question. Instead he went on, 'And you've kept yourself for me? You're a virgin?'

'I am, but it doesn't matter. James, who else should I lose my virginity to?'

Now he rolled onto his back, all bodily contact between them lost but for his hand which clutched hers. 'And you know we're destined to be together for ever. To be married, in fact… You've been told this by your voice that tells you when patients are really ill?'

Things were now dreadfully wrong. With her free hand she pulled the cover of the bed over her. She didn't want to be naked for this conversation. 'Perhaps married in time,' she faltered. 'But for now I just know we have to be together.'

He groaned. Then she felt him roll from the bed. When he spoke his voice was harsh at first, then became infinitely compassionate. But she didn't want compassion, she wanted love. 'Delyth, your voice is wrong. I'm very…fond of you. But any relationship I form will be temporary. I told you, I travel light. When I finish here I'll move on, perhaps to America—I'm already negotiating with Chicago. And I'll go alone. I've tried full-scale relationships, but they just don't work for me.'

'So you want me simply as a temporary lover?' she asked.

His reply was stark. 'Yes,' he said.

The silence between them seemed to stretch on for

ever. Then she said, 'If you'd go, I'd like to get dressed.'

The thing to do was not to feel anything. She had learned on the ward that if you tried hard enough you could distance yourself from your feelings. But this was harder.

She dressed, then looked quickly round the bare bedroom. It was now nearly dark. The sun had set. She walked out of the door. He, too, had dressed, and was sitting on the couch, his expression haggard. He stood quickly.

It was the hardest thing she had ever done, but she managed to keep her voice calm, her expression neutral. 'I can't talk now, James, but I know we'll have to say something some time. But, please, not now. I'm going home and I don't want you to walk with me.'

'I've hurt you, haven't I?' he asked.

'Yes,' she said, 'you have.'

CHAPTER FIVE

NEXT morning was dreadful. Usually when Delyth woke she looked forward to her work, to the day. Not this time. She woke late, as if her subconscious had told her that waking would bring the pain of remembrance. But somehow she tore herself out of bed.

Since she couldn't just forget what had happened, she forced herself to think about the night before, to decide what she felt, what she would have to do. As she drank her early morning cup of tea, sitting cross-legged on her bed, she wondered if she'd ever completely get over her rejection. Not that it had really been a rejection.

Surprisingly, she didn't feel ashamed or angry at herself. She knew she had perhaps acted in a forward way, had even led James on. But she'd done it sincerely. She thought she had *known* James was the only man for her. The fact that he didn't feel the same bewildered her.

She had to face the brutal fact. She had been wrong. James was not for her. She muttered it aloud, 'James doesn't love me, he doesn't love me, he doesn't want me.' Her dismay grew. What *could* she be certain of?

She remembered what Megan had said about James's face, about there being something hidden there. She had been right. James had turned his back on love, on all kinds of close relationships. She thought of his flat, so lacking any personal touch. What had he said? He wanted to travel light. That was both physically and emotionally. Well, that was his problem. She had parents, six sisters, no end of friends and relations. She knew what joy family closeness could bring—and, for that matter, what misery.

What was she going to do? She would have to work with him, see him regularly. It took a tremendous effort, but she told herself that she would handle it. She would not let this man make her miserable. A bit of her mind, which she tried to repress, said, Not much.

It wasn't hard to lose herself in work on the ward. She found herself talking to Wendy. She had been seen by an oncologist who thought they might have caught things in time. He had scheduled her for a lumpectomy the next day, and was cautiously optimistic about the prognosis. But Wendy was one of the world's great worriers. As she talked to Delyth she felt her breast almost constantly, as if holding it gave her comfort. Her hand was always inside her nightie.

'You must show me how to feel for lumps,' she told Delyth. 'Is there anywhere else I ought to feel?'

'Your breasts are the most important place,' Delyth told her, 'though you should also check for lumps in your neck. But there are other signs to look out for. If you cough up blood, or pass it vaginally, other than in your period, you should consult your doctor. If a mole changes, or you get non-healing sores on your skin, you should be concerned. And unexplained weight loss or persistent tiredness can be an indicator, too.' She could see Wendy carefully memorising all these pointers, and for a moment felt a pang of guilt. She guessed that Wendy's GP was going to see a lot of her in the future.

'Of course,' she went on, 'those are only vague indicators. Each of them might be explained by a dozen of things other than cancer.'

'Of course, Doctor,' Wendy said. 'Now, about the operation tomorrow. They have caught it in time, haven't they? I don't really need to worry?'

Delyth sighed. She wanted to reassure her patient, but she mustn't—she couldn't—tell her that all would be certainly well. 'Well, there's always a risk,' she began carefully, 'and no operation is ever a hundred per cent successful. But with any luck you should be fine. Incidentally, we'll do your varicose veins at the same time.'

Wendy laughed. 'I'd forgotten about them,' she said.

After her patients' round there was the massive amount of paperwork to attend to—the recommendations, the requests for tests, the preparations for admission and discharge, the letters to GPs. Delyth lost herself in this, working industriously in the doctors' room, and in the middle of the afternoon James came in.

She was sitting with her back to the door and when it clicked open, somehow she knew it was him. Her body tensed. He came to stand behind her, rested his hand on her shoulder a minute, then moved it. She could feel his reluctance to take his hand away. 'Hello, James,' she said, falsely bright. 'Where have you been keeping yourself?'

He didn't respond to her cheerfulness. Instead, he came to sit opposite her at the other side of the table. 'Did you get home all right last night?'

She considered the question, and decided not to let him off the hook. 'If you mean was I mugged or molested, the answer is no.'

Softly, he said. 'No, Delyth, that's not what I meant.' He looked at her, and as she stared back into his eyes she thought they'd never been so close and yet so distant. He had on that expression she'd come to think of as his stone face. It wasn't unpleasant, but gave no indication as to what he was thinking. His eyes were impenetrable.

He said, 'I've only known you for a while but in that time I've come to have a…high regard for you. But there's been a misunderstanding, and I think it's probably my fault. You want more of me than I'm capable of giving. I want to say I'm sorry.'

She shrugged. 'Perhaps we both made mistakes. You were very honest with me, and I don't think that a lot of men would have stopped when you did.'

The tiniest of smiles flicked across his lips. 'It wasn't easy,' he said.

'It wasn't easy for me either.' Her words were simple, and she realised they came nowhere near expressing what she really felt. Couldn't he also feel what there was—could be—between them? Apparently not. She had been so very wrong.

He went on, 'I came to tell you there's been a bit of a panic here. I was looking forward to at least working with you, and now it looks as if I can't.'

Inside her, she felt the stirrings of anger—and also of fear. 'I hope I haven't frightened you off,' she said, more viciously than she had intended. 'I do promise not to be an embarrassment to you.'

For a moment she saw anger flare in his eyes, and
wondered if she had gone too far. She knew what
depths of feeling he was capable of. But the anger died
and he shook his head. 'Nothing to do with you,
Delyth. Vic Adams, the S.R. at Lathom Street Hospital,
has tripped and broken his leg. They're short-staffed
there already so I'm to take over his work for a while.'

Lathom Street Hospital, she knew, was one of the
three smaller peripheral hospitals that shared some of
the facilities and staff with St Helen's. It was in the
suburbs, about ten miles away.

'So you won't be seen here so much?' she asked.

'No. And to save travel, I'm going to live on the job.
I'll take a couple of bags and sleep in the hospital.'

She couldn't help herself. 'You said you found it
very easy to move on. Didn't want to surround yourself
with—encumbrances.'

For a moment she thought she'd hurt him. He smiled
wryly. 'A good doctor knows all the pressure points,
where all the nerves are,' he said. 'I just wanted you
to know why you won't be seeing so much of me.'

'To say goodbye.'

He shook his head again. 'Not goodbye, Delyth. I
hope to come back soon. This is only *au revoir*.' He
stood and walked out of the room.

What did he mean by that? she asked herself. Then
she decided he'd meant nothing. They were just polite,
parting phrases. When he came back he would still be
her S.R. and she would learn a lot from him. They were
colleagues, nothing more. She had to keep reminding
herself of that.

She got up and made herself a cup of coffee at the

tiny kitchen in the corner. Only when she had drunk half of it did she realise she had put three spoonfuls of powder in her cup. It tasted undrinkable, yet she'd finished half of it. Was she going mad? She threw the rest away, rinsed her cup and made herself more. Then she concentrated on her work.

Half an hour later the door opened again. This time it was Matt. She was pleased to see him—she needed some simple, uncomplicated companionship. She had spent too much time with only her own thoughts.

'I've just dealt with a case of post-op hypotension,' he told her. 'Mrs Tennison had her appendicectomy this morning.'

'Serious?' she queried. A drop in blood pressure wasn't too unusual after general anaesthesia.

He shrugged. 'I don't think so. She seems well but a bit faint. Systolic blood pressure down just twenty millimetres. I've raised her legs and lowered her head, asked for her to be checked regularly.'

'Probably nothing,' she agreed.

The kettle was still warm and he made himself a coffee. 'Want another one?' he asked, pointing at her nearly empty cup. She didn't really, but she felt the need to share something with someone. And she liked Matt. He was simple, easy to be with. She nodded her assent.

'Heard about James going?' he asked her cautiously when they were sitting together at the table.

'Yes. He dropped in here a while ago.'

'We'll miss him. A bit frightening, but I think I've learned more from him than from Peter Kenny.'

'True,' she said, 'he's a good teacher.'

Matt sat silently, stirring his coffee far more than was necessary. 'You'll bore a hole in the bottom of your cup,' she pointed out.

He reddened a little, laid his spoon down and took a big mouthful of the hot liquid. Then he coughed and spluttered, and both of them laughed. 'Sorry,' he croaked, 'I was thinking of something else.'

'Going to tell me?'

The direct question seemed to throw him. He sipped more coffee, this time without spluttering. Then, with an obvious effort, he said, 'I thought you and James were getting quite…close.'

It was honest of him. But she wasn't going to be equally honest back. 'I like him a lot. But there's nothing…long term or serious between us.' Then, with more conviction than she really felt, she went on, 'In fact, there's nothing at all between us now.'

Matt was quick. '"Between us *now*"?' he questioned. 'You mean there was—?'

She wouldn't be cross-examined. 'I meant what I said,' she interrupted. 'Nothing between us apart from the fact that I like and admire him. Why d'you ask?'

'I want to take you out myself,' he blurted.

She looked at him in silence. He was tall, quite good-looking and for such a big man, appealing in a little-boy way. He was amiable, and she liked his company. But he wasn't James Owen.

And James Owen was nothing to her, she reminded herself.

'Look,' she said gently, 'we're both house officers, working ludicrous hours and taking what are, for us, big decisions. We've got no time for passion or heated relationships. We've just got to survive. I like you but I'm not ready for anything heavy.'

He persisted. 'So can I take you for a nice light-hearted drink tonight? Just you and me?'

'Do you *mean* light-hearted?' she questioned dubiously.

'Cross my heart, I do.'

'Then I'd love to go out with you.' When she saw the sheer delight on his face she felt a pang of guilt. I *have* warned him, she thought. What more can I do? And the idea of a simple uncomplicated evening was attractive.

She phoned Megan that night, just to chat and ask after Charles. After the usual exchanges Megan asked, 'And how're you and James?'

She should have known Megan would ask and wouldn't be put off. But Delyth intended to try. 'You sound like my big sister,' she said.

'I am your big sister and I take my big sisterly duties very seriously. You're avoiding the question so I already know the answer. What went wrong?'

She might as well be honest. She knew Megan would probe until she got the truth. 'We had a wonderful day. I thought we were getting on really well. Then he told me he just didn't want a...real relationship. He's not willing to give himself, wants to travel light.'

'Did he say why?'

Delyth thought she knew, but wasn't going to give Megan full details. 'He's had a...troubled life, Megan. He doesn't want more pain.'

'That shows in his face. How d'you feel, little sister?'

'I'll get over it.'

Thoughtfully Megan said, 'Delyth, perhaps he wasn't for you right now. But I want you to know that I like him and think an awful lot of him. What are you going to do now?'

'Go out with another hospital doctor,' Delyth said spiritedly.

Megan gulped with laughter. 'That's the idea. Fight back. Keep in touch and remember there're always other men.'

Delyth replaced the receiver. Did she want to fight back? Did she want another man?

In fact, it was four days before she could go out with Matt. She didn't see anything more of James—instead, she saw Peter Kenny and even Mr Forrester. Both took a ward round. Both were quite good, but they were slower and didn't have the same flair as James. Neither took her and Matt into the corridor and gave them a carefully worked-out list of things to think about. But she pressed on.

She saw quite a lot of Matt, of course, and noted with sad pleasure that he was more careful of her, more considerate now she had agreed to go out with him. When invited into her room he was more ready to leave when asked. When he asked her about going out he didn't do it in front of their other friends. She saw he didn't want to go out in a group. He wanted her to himself.

Both were now certain they could get out on

Tuesday night. On Monday night he said, 'There's this place called Palanquin. I thought we might have dinner there.'

She looked at him doubtfully. 'I read about it in the paper. Minor royalty and people out of *Vogue*.'

He was pleased she knew of it. 'Yes, that's the place. It should be good.'

She knew she'd have to choose her words carefully. 'Matt, I don't want you dressed up in your best suit and me in a long dress. I'd much rather have a quieter meal somewhere near and be back earlier. We've got to work on Thursday, you know, and we could be called in. Why not keep the posh place until we've got something to celebrate?'

He looked at her stonily. 'I can afford it, you know.'

'I know you can. But I'm not looking forward to going out to eat. I'm looking forward to going out with you. I couldn't relax at the Palanquin.'

It was the right thing to say, and his face relaxed. 'OK, we'll go somewhere closer.'

In the end one of the older doctors recommended him to an Italian restaurant in Covent Garden. Delyth had heard of it but had never been. They took a taxi there, had Parma ham, spaghetti with a seafood sauce and ice cream. The house wine was just fine. Then they walked along the Embankment, something she really liked. 'I love the lights,' she told him. 'They remind me of Llandudno and the River Conway.'

He laughed. 'You should see it where I live. Flat and desolate and dreary.'

'It's still the Thames. It's history.'

As they strolled along he took her hand. She let him.

He had been good company all night—she suspected he was deliberately suppressing the brasher side of his nature. He wanted to make an impression on her, wanted her to like him. The sad thought crept in that she would have been really happy if it hadn't been for her memories of James. Then she pushed the thought down.

When they got back to the residence they made tea and drank it in her room. When they had finished it he kissed her goodnight, not too passionately, and told her he wasn't going to try to stay. She told him she thought he was nice.

Over the next fortnight they went out quite regularly. They went to the jazz night again. Often they had to go out with Matt's group of friends, who seemed to expect it. Delyth was quite happy with this, Matt less so. 'Always with the gang,' he grumbled gently. 'I never seem to have you to myself.'

'Your fault for being so popular,' she reproved him. 'You've got lots of friends and I thought you liked going out in a group.'

He gave her a rueful smile. 'I'd rather be just with you.'

She was taking the bloods one morning when the junior nurse called her to the phone. 'It's Dr Owen for you,' she said. Delyth was glad of the warning. It gave her a chance to prepare herself. She was shocked at how her heart lurched at just the sound of his name. She was supposed to be getting over him!

Hearing his voice, it was worse. She hadn't heard

from him for nearly three weeks, but the pain came back in its entirety.

'Hello, Delyth, it's James. Work going OK? Are you coping with everything?' His voice was cautious.

'Plenty of work but I'm coping with it,' she said shakily.

'Coping with the work,' he muttered. 'Good.' Then he seemed to get a grip on what he was thinking and his voice became firmer. 'Delyth, I want a favour. If you can't do it, or don't want to, then please say so. I should be most upset if you did something that you might find…awkward.'

'I'll refuse if I want to,' she assured him. 'What do you want?'

'Peter Kenny suggested you and checked your roster. I phoned him first. You should be able to fit it in.'

She felt a vague sense of annoyance that James hadn't asked her directly for his favour, then put the feeling behind her. 'I'll do what I can. So, tell me, what is it?'

He sounded almost embarrassed. 'It's silly really. You know I'm a runner when I get time? Well, the club I run with is putting on a half-marathon next Sunday, round one of the parks in North London. We've got quite a lot taking part. St John's Ambulance people will be helping us, but the doctor we had on site has let us down. Can you do it?'

It was an unusual request. 'I don't know much about sports injuries,' she told him. 'What will I be expected to do?'

'Probably not a lot. The committee just felt they wanted a doctor handy, and our insurance company asks for it. If you don't do it then I shall have to. So I'm asking you to spoil your Sunday afternoon so I can enjoy mine.'

'I'd like to do it,' she told him, 'and it won't spoil my afternoon. But just remember that I've never dealt with sports injuries or exhaustion before.'

He seemed relieved. 'You'll be working with people who know more about it than you do, and you'll probably enjoy learning something. But we need a doctor as a last line of defence—heart attack or something like that. There'll be a mini-treatment room set up by the sports pavilion. You don't need to organise or bring anything except a white coat.'

'I'll be there. Give me the address.'

He didn't ring off after giving her the details she needed. Instead, there was a pause. 'I'm…glad I feel that I can ask a favour of you,' he said eventually, 'and I'm glad that you're willing to do it.'

'You should know that I'd do a lot more for you than this,' she said bitterly, and rang off. She was suffering. Let him suffer too.

Mid-morning on Sunday she took a train to a distant London suburb. James had left her a message offering to pick her up. She had left him a reply saying it wasn't necessary. She quite enjoyed her long trip, trundling through new bits of the city.

She was always surprised at the amount of parkland there was in London. As she walked from the station to the park she knew she was on the right road as there were young men and women in tracksuits trotting past her. Eventually she found the park and was directed to the sports pavilion.

There was a marquee to one side of the pavilion. She entered to be greeted by the evocative scent of cut grass, canvas and embrocation. And there was James coming towards her, dressed in an old blue tracksuit, the jacket open to show the thin singlet underneath.

She wasn't prepared for the sudden rush of longing she felt. She'd thought she had her feelings well under control—now she discovered she didn't. She loved him! Even if he didn't love her.

He was looking at her cautiously. Perhaps something of what she felt showed in her face. She forced herself to smile at him.

'I'm glad you could come, Delyth,' he said. 'It's purely selfish. If you're here I can take part in the run.'

'A man must have his exercise,' she told him, and he had the grace to look uncomfortable.

'Afterwards I could drive you back to the hospital,' he said. 'Perhaps on the way we might—'

'There's no need, I've got a return ticket. But you can show me what my duties are here.'

He looked at her stone-face, then apparently realised that it was going to be strictly business between them. 'Of course. All the first aid is run by John Williams here. You'll find him very experienced, very friendly.'

John Williams turned out to be a bright-eyed, bearded man in his late fifties, an obvious enthusiast. He introduced her to his team. They didn't seem to resent Delyth at all, but when James had gone she felt she had to make some excuse.

'I doubt I'll be able to do anything as well as you,'

she said. 'I've only been a doctor for a few weeks so give me any job you want. I have worked as a nurse. I'm very happy to bandage sprains and see to cuts.'

He beamed at her. 'That's a very generous offer. I always wanted to be a doctor myself, but I had to leave school to go into insurance and this has been my hobby for the past forty years. We don't usually need a doctor, but when we do we need one badly. We'll be glad of your help.'

He glanced at his watch. 'There's little to do here now. Why don't you go and watch the race start? It'll be in ten minutes.'

Once outside she realised it was a well-organised event. About five hundred were taking part, and were carefully martialled in stages. The first stretch of the race was across the park where there was plenty of open ground. The runners would space themselves, before making a second circuit and out onto the road. There was the countdown on the PA system, then the great line of runners moved forward. At first they seemed just a solid mass, but soon they broke up as the faster runners streaked ahead.

She didn't see James. But she waited for ten minutes until the leaders had reached the top of the park and come running back. Then she saw him. He wasn't with the first group, but was lying about twenty-fifth. She didn't want him to see her, and so she stood in the shade of a tree. He was dressed in blue shorts and a white singlet. Now she realised why he walked so fast. His legs were long and he seemed to stride effortlessly. And on his face was a curious expression, half contentment, half determination. Delyth went back to the tent.

'There'll be a few with exhaustion,' John told her. 'There're always one or two who haven't quite trained hard enough but think it doesn't matter. Fortunately it's not too hot, otherwise we'd have some with heat prostration—that can get quite nasty. Had to send one or two to hospital in the past. Blisters, of course, cuts and scratches when people fall over, occasional sprains. But there'll be nothing for an hour or so so we'll all have a coffee.'

There was a rustling at the marquee door behind them, the sobbing of a child. 'Please, is there a doctor here?' an anguished voice called.

Delyth thought it polite to let John look at the case first. He moved over to where a young mother was clutching a wailing child, and led them both gently to a bed. Delyth followed him. When she saw the blood on the child's sleeve she didn't need John's beckoning arm to tell her that she was needed.

'He was playing on the wall by the trees,' the woman sobbed, 'and he fell off against this fence. There was a big nail sticking out and it dragged right down his arm.'

John was efficiently cutting off the little boy's shirt sleeve, a pad held against the still bleeding wound. Delyth pulled on a pair of rubber gloves. 'What's your little boy's name?' she asked gently. 'Are you his mother?'

'Yes, I'm Debbie Wright and this is Wayne. He's

just seven. Is he going to be all right? Look at all the blood!'

John looked at Delyth, then waved over one of his assistants. 'Go and sit down a minute, Debbie, and we'll get you a hot drink. When you feel better come and hold Wayne's hand.' Debbie was led away, and John and Delyth bent over the whimpering little boy.

It didn't take either of them long to make a decision. Carefully Delyth wiped away the blood from the long cut and eased out a couple of obvious pieces of rusty metal. She looked at John and shook her head. 'It's beyond me here and with this equipment. He'll have to go to A and E. I think there may be some deep tissue damage. We'll just put a pad on and phone for an ambulance.'

He smiled at her. 'I'm glad you said that. You're the doctor, but it looks to me like a job that's going to take a consultant. I'll keep him warm and talk to him. You go and tell his mother what's happening.'

Debbie wasn't as happy with the decision. The sweet tea and biscuits had cheered her up considerably. 'You're a doctor, aren't you?' she asked. 'Why can't you stitch him up?'

'I want someone more expert than me to look at that cut,' Delyth said carefully. 'It might need specialist attention.'

'I knew something like this would happen when we came to the park. That one's always in trouble. And I was going to go out tonight.'

'Come and put your arm round him,' Delyth said. 'The ambulance will soon be here.'

In fact, it was remarkably quick. Delyth wrote a

quick note to the A and E staff and said goodbye to their now silent little charge. Debbie climbed into the ambulance and said nothing.

John winked at Delyth. 'Don't expect thanks every time,' he said.

After that there were the first casualties from the race. The organisers had arranged for there to be cars waiting around the route. They now brought in those who were in trouble. There was nothing too serious, as John had said—a few blisters and a man who had sprained his ankle slipping off the pavement.

Then there was a potentially more serious case. An older man, George Norris, was brought in—she guessed he'd be in his late forties. He was showing obvious signs of distress, complaining of dizziness and nausea. 'I was doing so well,' he told her, 'up there with people half my age.'

'Very good,' she told him. 'Do you train regularly?'

It turned out that he hadn't been running as often as he used to. 'But I'm still as good as I always was. Plenty of running in me still. I was doing fine, then suddenly—I couldn't go on any more.'

'Just lie still, Mr Norris,' she told him. 'There's a couple of things we want to check.'

Both pulse and breathing were rapid, even though he'd stopped running twenty minutes before. His face was pale and clammy. One of the men who had brought him in said that George had been sitting by the roadside and that when he'd tried to stand he'd temporarily lost consciousness. Syncope, she thought—not enough blood pressure.

'Did you have much to drink as you ran, Mr Norris?'

'Don't hold with it. I always lose weight when I run. Good for you.'

'In your case, I'm not so sure.' She told him to drink what he could and rest on the cot provided. She would check on him again in a few minutes. 'Quite frankly, I think you've overdone it,' she told him. 'You're exhausted. Before you do any more running you're to see your GP and get a thorough check-up.'

'I've never felt as bad as this before. I will.'

There was another lull. 'The first runners are in sight,' John told her. 'D'you want to go and watch the finish? It's only a few yards from here. If we need you we'll send for you.'

She was tempted, and gave in. 'I'd like to watch,' she said, 'but, please, do send for me if there's anything I can do.' She took off her white coat and walked over to where the finishers would be channelled into lines.

The first man sprinted up to the line. He was small, thin, hardly an ounce of fat on him. He held up his arm to acknowledge the cheers of the spectators. After him there was a bunch of a twenty or so, and then she saw James. Her heart beat faster. She had to admit to herself that she hadn't come out to watch the end of the race. She'd come to see James.

His singlet and shorts were soaked with sweat, his hair streaked with it. He was in a group of four men. As they neared the finishing line three of them tried to sprint and pulled away from James. She saw the rictus of strain on his face as he forced unwilling muscles to pump faster. His chest heaving, he caught up with them. The crowd saw the little personal competition and began to shout. All four ran faster. But somehow

James managed to creep ahead and hold his tiny lead until he ran first into the finishing alley. She saw him collect his place card, trot slowly for another few yards, finally stop and bow his head to his knees.

She walked over to him. 'Congratulations,' she said. 'You nearly killed yourself in the last few yards to come thirty-first instead of thirty-fourth.' Then she smiled to show she didn't mean it.

'Trust a woman to hit a man when he's down,' he gasped. 'How has your afternoon been?'

'I've enjoyed it and learned a few things. But we've been largely trouble-free.' She paused a minute. 'What are you doing?'

He was bent over, his leg straight, the toe pointing upwards. 'Stretching the muscles and tendons,' he told her. 'If you do this after every race you won't get stiff.' He changed position to stretch the other leg.

'I must remember that.' She could smell, feel, the maleness of him. Curiously she asked, 'You enjoyed pushing yourself to the limit, didn't you?'

'If you don't push yourself, it's not worth doing. Delyth, thanks again for giving me the chance of running.'

'I'd better get back to the tent,' she said.

The tent was filling up. John told her that some of the runners just came in to lie down. They didn't exactly feel ill but they wanted to rest in comfort. She looked at one or two minor problems, checked a couple of people who looked slightly more ill. And she found George Norris, sitting up on his cot, eagerly talking to another runner.

'I feel much better, Doctor,' he told her eagerly. 'I

think I know where I went wrong. It won't happen the next time I—'

'Look,' she told him, 'you have to see your GP. What happened to you can be serious. Next time it might not be a simple drink and a rest.' She took his pulse. 'Now, lie down for another half-hour.'

'I know what my GP will say. Stop running. Take up something stupid like golf instead.'

'If your heart goes into fibrillation—starts beating irregularly—you could dislodge a small blood clot. If it reaches the brain the consequences of that are far worse than a rest in a medical tent. We're talking about a stroke, possible paralysis. All I'm saying is talk to your GP. Otherwise you might be sorry.'

'Will he do as he's told?' she asked John a few minutes later.

John looked thoughtful. 'Possibly,' he said, 'though a lot of these men are fanatics.'

'You're telling me. I've met some.'

It was unfortunate that James should pick that moment to walk up behind them. He had heard what she'd said but he looked at her expressionlessly. He was in his old blue tracksuit again and she noticed that he'd washed his face and hair.

'I can take over from you now, Delyth,' he said, 'unless you want to stay a bit longer with me?'

She shook her head. 'I think I'll go back to the hospital. Thank you for the chance to work with the group. I've found it very interesting and I think I've learned something. But there's nothing else for me here.'

He knew what she meant. As she turned to go she saw the anger in his eyes again. But he'd had his chance. She just wasn't interested in a casual relationship.

'Once again, thank you for all you've done,' he said harshly.

'It was nothing.' She turned to John Williams, her voice consciously more pleasant. 'I've enjoyed being here, John. Hope to see you again some time.'

'You'll always be welcome,' he assured her.

She was aware of the two men looking at her back as she walked across the park, and wondered miserably if they were talking about her. This had not been a good idea. She had thought she would be professional with James, one colleague helping another. Instead, all her previous pains had resurfaced. Did he have *no* feelings for her? Didn't he know what he had just made her suffer? He was harder, darker than she had thought.

CHAPTER SIX

'WHERE have you been? I've been looking for you.'

It was too bad that the first person Delyth had to meet when she entered the residence was Matt. He'd had a morning shift. It was now about half past five, and she hadn't enjoyed the trip back half as much as she'd enjoyed the trip out. She rather resented his question, but knew this was nothing to do with him. She was the ill-tempered one.

For a moment she considered hiding the truth, then decided not to. It had been her decision to go. 'I've been doctor in charge at a half-marathon in north London,' she told him.

He looked away. He knew about James's hobby. 'You've been out with James Owen,' he accused her.

She wondered why she had to justify herself to him, but she knew he meant well. 'I haven't been out with him. I did him a favour,' she said soothingly. 'In fact, I enjoyed myself and I came straight back.'

'Not going out with him?'

'Why should I? Anyway, he didn't ask me.' It wasn't quite a lie.

Matt appeared to be placated by this. 'So you're still coming to the jazz with us tonight?'

'I'm looking forward to it,' she told him honestly.

She did enjoy the jazz at the Old City Walls that night. She was with a group of friends and they had a happy, noisy time. Back at the residence there was a bustling party, shouting and singing, drinking tea and making cheese on toast. But they all had to work the next day and it soon ended.

She found herself in her bedroom with Matt. When she sat on her bed he came to sit beside her and kissed her, gently at first. She was happy with this and kissed him back. But his kisses became more passionate, more demanding. She felt his hand stray down her front and cautiously stroke her breast. She didn't really object, but...she had to be fair. Gently, she pushed away his hand and took his arms from round her.

'You can kiss me in my bedroom, Matt, and I quite like it,' she said. 'But I'll tell you now I don't want to go any further. We've both got enough to think about now without that. I like you, I'm sorry, but that's how it is.'

He smiled sheepishly, then kissed her again, a soft, almost brotherly kiss. 'That's fine by me,' he said. 'I like you a lot, Delyth. I think you're worth waiting for. We'll get to know each other more and see what happens.'

It was a generously spirited remark and she liked him more for it. Quickly kissing him on the cheek, she said, 'What happens now is that we both get some sleep. Go to bed. I'll give you a shout in the morning.' Smiling, he left.

She was tired now—she was always tired—but she couldn't sleep. As she lay in bed she thought about her life and the two men in it. Or the one man in it?

'I'm a typical Essex man,' Matt had said. But he

wasn't. Now he was turning from a brash young person into someone who was hard-working and attractive. There was sensitivity there, she thought, and a genuine caring for her. Would she come to love him?

This she didn't know. She thought she might, but as yet there had been no blinding flash, no absolute conviction that this was the man for her. The odd power that she sometimes had was not there to be tapped or referred to—it struck when it wished. And it had been so wrong about James. She just didn't know if Matt could be the man for her.

What about James? She realised now how little she had thought about him since that wonderful afternoon and that appalling evening. It was as if her mind had blanked him off as being too painful to consider.

The two men's faces flashed before her. Matt, handsome, open and friendly. James as he had been earlier today, sweat-streaked, grim and determined, even in some pain. There was a darkness about James that wasn't present in Matt. The sad conviction grew that James was still part of her life. She didn't know how, but somehow he was going to affect her. She shivered. It might be for the bad.

A week later she was sitting in the doctors' room on the ward, wrestling again with her paperwork. This time it was a set of TTOs—To Take Out forms. Often these were dealt with by someone senior, but she'd been asked to handle a few. They were the forms that patients took with them when they were discharged, and which entitled the patients to drugs from the hospital pharmacy. As ever, there was an awful lot of copying to be done.

James walked in. She was shocked. She hadn't seen him since the race, and before that hadn't seen him for three weeks, but after all this time her body still reacted to his closeness. Her heart beat faster and she knew her face coloured slightly. She missed him! By this time surely she was entitled to a little peace? She *had* to get over him.

He looked tired. In the past she had thought him impervious to the strains all the rest of them felt, but now there were lines by his eyes, a deepening in the creases by his mouth. He still looks gorgeous, an impertinent part of her mind suggested, and she struggled to push the thought away.

'You look as if you've been having a hard time,' she said. She hadn't intended to be so personal, so concerned, when they first met again, but the words just slipped out.

'They've been working me hard at Lathom Street. There was a bit of a backlog of operations. I tried to get it down. Mostly just run-of-the-mill stuff—varicose veins and so on. Still, they cause enough misery. Did a gastrectomy yesterday—some poor devil with a bleeding ulcer in his stomach. Anyway, they've got a replacement now so I've got a couple of days off then I'm back here. How have you been?'

'Busy. Just the usual, but I think I'm learning. I'm enjoying the work.'

'It's good to concentrate,' he agreed.

'It certainly takes your mind off other things,' she said acidly, then cursed herself silently. He'd tried to offer her a reasonable, boring conversation about work, something they could build a professional relationship on. And she'd wrecked it. She looked up, rather shame-faced, and found him grinning at her.

'All good doctors have a reservoir of toughness,' he said. 'They have to be able to defend themselves. *You* take the fight into the enemy camp.'

Now she *was* embarrassed. She was desperately try-ing to think of some flippant remark when the phone rang. He picked it up, listened, offered it to her. 'For you.'

'Dr Price here,' she barked, grateful for any respite. At first she didn't recognise the voice on the other end of the line. It was low, possibly drugged, and there was the catch of pain in it. 'Megan!' she gasped. 'Are you all right?'

'I've been better,' her sister said. 'I'm just realising that there might be something good about having a doctor in the family.'

'What happened? Are you ill?'

There was the sound of Megan trying to laugh. 'Not ill, injured. I'm trying to persuade myself that it's a joke. I fell off a stool in the kitchen, Delyth. And I was standing on tiptoe. Anyway, I sprained my ankle. Not just an ordinary sprain, but a tendon-tearing good job. I was in agony, and the A and E officer I saw said it was worse than if I'd broken it.'

'How did you get to hospital?' Delyth broke in. She knew what absolute pain a sprained ankle could cause.

'I lay on the floor and phoned for Charles next door. He let himself in and called an ambulance. Anyway, the thing is, I'm largely immobilised and since I can't work I thought I'd have a bit of home comfort. I'm going back to Mum's cooking. But I don't fancy the train journey, and I certainly can't drive, so I wondered if you could drive me there on your next free day.'

'Of course I'll drive you,' Delyth said at once, 'and, in fact, I'm off tomorrow.'

'Super! You haven't got a car. We'll take my old Land Rover.'

'The Land Rover? Fine,' Delyth said doubtfully. The thing was, she wasn't a very confident driver. She'd passed her test, of course, but after that she hadn't had much practice. And Megan's heavy vehicle wasn't the Mini she'd learned in. Still, she'd cope. 'I want to get an early start. I'll be round at yours about half past six in the morning,' she told her sister, and replaced the receiver.

'I'll drive you both,' a voice said.

She turned to look at James. 'Why should you?' she asked.

'Because I've got the day off and nothing much to do. Because I very much fancy a trip into Wales. Because I drove a Land Rover all the time in Africa. Because I could tell by your face that you weren't really looking forward to driving, and I need my junior staff to stay happy.'

They were all good reasons and not one of them was the one she wished to hear. For a moment she thought about asking Matt, but she knew he was on duty. And being driven by someone was preferable to driving herself so... 'That's very kind of you,' she said. 'I'll accept.'

*   *   *

Megan had borrowed crutches from the hospital and could hobble a few feet, but James picked her up effortlessly and carried her downstairs. He established her in a nest of blankets and pillows on the back seat of her tatty old diesel Land Rover. Then he went to fetch her cases.

Megan hadn't apparently been surprised when James had turned up with Delyth. 'Has your affair restarted, then?' she asked while James was upstairs. 'Not that I'm objecting. I like him and I'm glad of his help.'

'We haven't restarted anything. He just wanted a trip into Wales.'

'Of course he did. D'you think Mum will like him? You have warned her, haven't you?'

'I phoned to say a colleague had offered to drive us,' Delyth said stiffly.

'I'll bet she gets the best china out.'

Then James returned, Delyth strapped herself into the front seat and they were off.

She might have guessed that James was a good driver. He drove as he operated, quickly and decisively, threading his way through the morning London traffic. She thought it typical of him that he had checked the road map and memorised the route out of the city. She would have got there eventually, but it seemed no time before they were on the slip road to the M1, driving north.

'I love driving Land Rovers,' he told them. 'I had one of my own in Africa. When I had an hour to spare—which was practically never—I used to drive out into the bush. No roads, for once no patients—just me, the bush and solitude.'

'And insects,' Megan put in from the back.

He laughed. 'Oh, yes, indeed, the insects. Who could forget them?'

He accelerated when they were on the motorway. The diesel engine was noisy and it wasn't too easy to talk. Megan was still in some pain. Delyth had given her a couple of powerful analgesics, and she quickly dozed off. 'I could take over for a bit, if you like,' she shouted to James.

'I'm enjoying myself, don't worry. Why don't you doze too? Your seat will recline.'

She had one quick glance at his profile. He was absorbed in his driving, half smiling, his eyes calculating what was happening ahead. So he didn't want to talk to—shout at—her. Very well. It was his decision. After all, she was tired and it had been an early start. She would get some sleep. She pulled at the lever that caused her seat to fall back.

She must have been more tired than she'd realised. The next thing she remembered was being gently shaken. 'I can see the hills of Wales in the distance,' he said. 'Want to wake and have a look?'

She struggled awake. 'Where are we?'

'Just come off the M54. We're on the A5 now. Soon be at Shrewsbury.'

'That far! We're past Birmingham. I've been asleep for hours!'

'Sleep while you can. I do. Are you glad to be going home?'

They were less than an hour from her village. She felt a certain excitement, but... 'I'm partly glad,' she said. 'I've spent most of my life in rural Wales and I love it. But London's been good for me. Perhaps I was getting a bit parochial—a bit narrow.'

'What will you do when you finish your house jobs, Delyth? What's your future career to be?'

This was a good question. After pondering, she said, 'Until recently all I wanted was to be a Welsh GP. I worked a lot with our local one, Alun Roberts. He helped me and I supposed I wanted to be like him. But now…well, I am enjoying hospital work.' She paused for a moment and then said, 'There aren't many female surgeons, are there?'

'Not many,' he agreed, 'but some, and those I have worked with have been very good. Now, where do we go from here?'

The hills were closer now, and at her direction they turned off the main highway. Then they were in a maze of tiny roads, known to her since she was a child, threading their way round hills and past farms. Behind them Megan sat up, wakened by the swaying as they negotiated more and more tight bends. Then they were in the village where she'd grown up. There was the post office, the bakery, the tiny primary school, the single pub. It was an odd sensation. It wasn't the same as when she'd been away at university. Then she'd known she'd be coming back. Now…perhaps she had left for good.

Finally they turned into the drive of the house. Behind it she could see the long gleaming lines of her father's greenhouses. Her mother came to the door, warned by the crunch of the tyres on the gravel. Then it hit her. It was *good* to be home!

*   *   *

Her father was away, giving a paper at a conference on market gardening and its place in the rural economy. 'He was dreading it,' her mother said cheerfully, 'but he phoned last night and said some of the people there actually knew what they were talking about. There's talk of part of a television programme being shot down here.'

'The village will like that,' said Megan, now lying on the couch.

'Will Grandad be on the telly?' asked Robert, one of Delyth's numerous nephews and nieces. Her sister Lucie was a music teacher who had married a local farmer, and she'd brought her three children over for the day.

'He might,' said Lucie. 'Why?'

'I help Grandad dig sometimes,' said four-year-old Robert. 'And weed and carry things. Will I be on telly, too?'

'You can sit on the draining board and help me with the peas,' Delyth's mother said, picking up her grandson. 'And don't eat so many this time.'

Lucie winked at Delyth and James. 'He spends more time here in the garden than he does watching television,' she said. 'Strange child. Sometimes I worry about him. Now, Delyth, never mind the medicine—are you getting any singing done?'

James had been introduced and quietly accepted. He sat in the giant rocking chair, watching Delyth and her family. After an hour they all went to the giant conservatory for lunch. It was still warm enough to eat out there.

'We call it a conservatory,' Delyth told James as

they arranged themselves round the trestle table, 'but, as you can see, really it's just another of my father's greenhouses.' She waved at the neatly arrayed growing plants.

'My husband's a lucky man, Dr Owen,' her mother told James. 'His job is his hobby.'

'I think he's lucky in more ways that that,' James said, 'and will you call me James?'

It was a good lunch—fresh salad from the greenhouses, their own eggs, bread baked that morning and ham from the local butcher. Delyth had almost forgotten what really fresh food was like. The hospital canteen did very well, she supposed, but it was nothing like home cooking.

After the meal Mrs Owen turned to James and said, 'You've driven all the way here and I gather you're going to do all the driving back. If I know my two daughters, they slept most of the journey. Would you like to go into the study with your tea and catnap for an hour? You'll find it refreshing and I'll see you're not disturbed.'

He smiled at her. 'You should have been a surgeon's wife. That's a great idea.'

So James slept while Delyth, her mother, Lucie and her two children wandered round the greenhouses. There was a lot of family gossip to catch up on, a lot to tell about her new job. And it was good to feel the damp heat of the greenhouses, to smell and inspect the growing plants.

'He seems a nice man, this James,' her mother said. 'You say you're working for him?'

'He's the specialist registrar on my firm,' Delyth answered cautiously. 'He does a lot of the teaching.'

'Tell him if he ever wants a few days' break he can come and stay a while,' her mother said. 'I'd like to see him again.'

And that was all. Delyth smiled to herself. She should have known that she wouldn't be questioned on anything. Her mother knew instinctively what needed saying, what could be left unsaid. Her mother liked him.

When they returned to the house Lucie ordered Delyth to the main living room. 'It's the other end of the house from the study,' she said, 'and we won't disturb the sleeping doctor. I haven't heard you sing for six months. It's wicked!'

Megan hauled herself onto her crutches. 'I'm coming too,' she announced. 'I might even join in.'

Delyth blinked. But this had always been a house full of singing voices, and she realised it was another thing she had missed.

The house walls were solid, and they were some way from the study. James would sleep on. Lucie seated herself at the piano and played a couple of chords. 'Right,' she said, 'you know this.'

'This' was 'Bye-bye, Blackbird'. They had all sung it as children together, and she loved it. After it was finished they all sang 'In the Good Old Summertime' and then, more difficult, she sang 'September Song' alone.

It was now nearly the end of September.

'"When the autumn weather turns the leaves to

flame, one hasn't got time for the waiting game'','
Delyth sang.

Her eyes closed as she moved towards the end. It
always seemed to her one of the finest, saddest songs
she knew.

There was silence as she finished. And then someone
clapped. She opened her eyes to see James in the doorway. How long had he been there? Why hadn't she
heard him arrive?

'That was truly lovely,' he told her gravely. 'But
your mother sent me to tell you it's time we were moving.'

It made sense, of course. It was a long journey back
and she had to be at work next morning. They had a
farewell coffee, her mother stuffed a vast bag of sandwiches in the car, kisses all round and they were away.

'How d'you feel?' he asked her as they finally drove
out of the well-loved village. 'Sorry to be leaving?'

She considered the question. 'Half-sorry. I grew up
there. I have so many good memories, of family and
friends. But I've started on a new path now. I'm learning to be a doctor. I'm looking forward to being at
work tomorrow morning.'

She didn't tell him she was slightly apprehensive
about the next few hours. How would she manage in
his company?

'It was very good of you to drive us,' she said. 'I
suppose I could have managed, but you made it all
seem so much easier.'

'I'm enjoying it. And it was a very pleasant break.'
He pulled out to slide expertly around a lorry. 'And I

did enjoy meeting your family. I can see the attraction of having so many people caring for you.'

'But you still don't want one of your own?' It slipped out before she had a chance to stop herself. Why did she have to ask something so stupid?

'I can manage,' he replied bleakly. 'I've made my decision and I'll stick to it.'

She could think of no answer to that.

CHAPTER SEVEN

DELYTH knew Mary Cooney was going to be a squeamish patient. Mary was young, tried to act tough, but there had been fear in her eyes as she'd looked at the IV lines dripping into the arms of other patients. 'You're going to cut a hole in my arm? Put one of those things inside it?'

'We have to put drugs straight into your bloodstream,' Delyth explained. 'It's a bit uncomfortable but it doesn't really hurt.' She could tell by the rigidity of her patient's body that Mary didn't believe her so she smeared EMLA anaesthetic cream over the selected veins and left a dressing over it for half an hour. Now there should be no feeling at all.

Mary was right-handed so Delyth picked a vein in the left arm in the cubital fossa, the hollow just in front of the elbow joint. She tightened the tourniquet about the arm. 'Don't look if you don't want,' she suggested to Mary. Mary squeezed her eyes shut.

Delyth eased the needle through the skin and subcutaneous fat, then felt the resistance give way as she pierced the vein. A drop or two of blood appeared in the base of the cannula, the tube that would be inserted into the vein. Then it was simply a matter of gently withdrawing the metal stylet which had done the actual cutting and advancing the plastic cannula further into the vein. It was done. She secured the cannula to the arm with a dressing, and took off the tourniquet. 'All done,' she told Mary. 'We can give you a drip now.'

'Nothing to it,' Mary said.

Matt was in the doctors' room. 'Good day yesterday?' he asked pleasantly.

'I went back home for the day. My sister hurt her ankle and James Owen drove us both to my parents'.'

She could tell by the stillness of his shoulders that this wasn't the best news he'd ever heard. 'I thought you and James had fallen out,' he said. He managed to keep his voice neutral, but she knew what he was thinking.

'We get on together—we have to. I would have asked you to drive, but I knew you couldn't take the time off. So I was pleased when James offered to help.'

'And where does that leave me?' He was still trying to control his anger—she appreciated that.

She walked round the table to kiss him on the cheek. 'It leaves you as a hard-working house officer and a good friend of mine,' she said. 'Now, have you looked at those radiography referral forms?'

There was never time for long soul-searching sessions during the day. They were too busy. But just for a moment she wondered why she had to explain her actions to Matt. Then she found herself wondering if, had things been different, she would have wanted to explain things to James. There was no answer so she got on with her work.

Mid-morning, a call came up from A and E. 'Got you another client, an awkward one, Delyth. Doesn't speak a word of English. Apparently the police were called to a fight of some sort, and when they got there only this man was left. His pals deserted him. Police sent for an ambulance and have left us to sort things out. We don't know who he is, there's nothing at all in his pockets and we don't even know what language he speaks.'

Delyth grimaced. So much of her time was taken up with paperwork. The prospect of dealing with someone who couldn't offer a single fact filled her with horror. This could take for ever. 'Why are you we admitting him?' she asked.

'The usual contusions and bruises, but I doubt they're too important. He's had some kind of heavy blow to the head. We need to observe him for a couple of days. We've given him a skull CT—there's nothing too serious showing on it.'

Delyth nodded to herself. Computerised tomography, a form of X-ray, would reveal a lot of possible damage. Perhaps this patient wouldn't be too troublesome. 'Send him up,' she said. 'I'll see about a bed.'

The new patient was brought up on a trolley, his clothes in a basket at the bottom, his notes to hand. Delyth had him taken into a side ward, swished the curtains round and looked at the form she had to fill in. For the moment much of it would have to remain blank.

'I'll call you John,' she said, smiling at the dark man below her. 'That is, unless you can tell me your name?'

John was now conscious, his large eyes flashing, obviously frightened. But he didn't respond to her invitation. With a young nurse in attendance, Delyth carried out a full examination, explaining to the nurse what she was doing. She got rather a kick out of being a teacher for once, rather than a student.

There were tribal scars on John's cheeks, but they meant nothing to Delyth. She found John to be a youngish man, thin but not emaciated. He had been badly knocked about in the fight and there were several injuries that were obviously painful, but which she didn't think life-threatening. Delyth paid particular attention to the bruising to the chest. 'It's important to ensure there are no fractures or visceral injuries,' she explained to the young nurse. 'They might lead to hypotension—low blood pressure—and that can compound any brain damage.' But in this case she was reasonably sure there was no great damage.

She took blood and had it sent down for the blood gases to be checked, then went to look for Peter Kenny. She knew he was on the ward somewhere. Head injuries should always be referred to someone senior, she had been told.

Peter Kenny looked at her notes, and the patient, and decided there was no need to send for a neurosurgeon. 'Keep him under observation,' he said. 'Any serious deterioration, let me know. But I don't feel his injuries are too serious. Pity he can't talk to us.'

'Who d'you think he is?' Delyth asked.

Peter shrugged. 'Probably an illegal immigrant. This isn't our problem. You mustn't get involved, Delyth. Concentrate on the medical aspect. We just don't have the resources for social investigations.'

'Can we separate the two?'

'No,' he said, 'we can't. But we have to.'

She knew Peter was right, his apparent hardness was just a self-protecting mechanism. She'd have to develop it herself in time. But at present it was difficult.

The hospital had come across the problem of non-English speakers before. At intervals through the day people came onto the ward to try to speak to John in their native languages. St Helen's was a cosmopolitan hospital, and there were people there from many nationalities. But John responded to none of them. Delyth watched as one man spoke in a curious hissing language, and was sure there was the flash of intelligence on John's face. But he didn't reply.

'I thought he understood me, miss,' the man said. He was a worker in the boiler room. 'But I couldn't get him to talk back.'

'Well, thanks for trying,' she said.

John's case was only one of several she had to deal with. She turned to something else.

Next morning she was in the operating theatre, assisting Mr Forrester. This was work she thoroughly enjoyed, though Forrester was not quite as ready as James to let her try the simpler techniques. He was performing an aortic aneurysm repair. The wall of the aorta, the main artery of the heart, had stretched and become weakened, and it was necessary to replace a section of it with a man-made tube. Delyth practised suturing under his careful attention. Once again she wondered about being a surgeon herself, but decided this was not a good time to mention it.

When she got back on the ward after the morning's work, her mysterious patient had gone.

'His uncle came for him,' Matt explained. 'He was

very polite, insisted that John could sign himself out. Apparently he's going to be a student here. I wasn't very keen on letting him go, but the uncle knew all the ropes. There was no way I could keep him here. I couldn't section him.'

Delyth frowned. 'What sort of man was this uncle?'

Matt shrugged. 'Like I said, always polite but obviously used to getting his own way. Quite well dressed, but he had two full gold teeth in the front. You don't often see those now. Said he'd bring John back to Outpatients. I got him to sign, and put his address underneath.'

He showed her the form that had been signed. And as she looked at it something struck her with the force of a nightmare. John was going to die. Worse than that... What was it? Worse than that... The room spun around her. She had never had a feeling as bad as this before.

She felt Matt's arm round her shoulder, felt him guide her to a chair. 'Are you OK, Delyth? You look faint.' She heard the concern in his voice.

'Yes, I'm fine. I'm just a bit...worried about this man.' She had told James about the power she had, but had never thought of telling Matt. For a moment she wondered why. Anyway, she certainly wasn't going to start now.

'We just can't go into people's personal problems,' Matt said, kindly enough, 'and certainly not if they don't invite us to.'

'We're supposed to treat the whole person!'

'It's just not always possible. Now, d'you want to go back to your room to rest? I can cope with what's left here.' She knew he was being considerate, but that wasn't what she wanted.

'I'm all right. A quick coffee and I'll be back on the ward.' She had work to do.

That evening she had intended to sit quietly in her room, perhaps do a bit of background reading. But at half past eight she found she couldn't rest. Throwing on a coat, she went and climbed in one of the taxis that waited outside the hospital gates. She gave the driver the address the gold-toothed man had given as John's home—she just couldn't forget it.

It wasn't a long journey. The address didn't exist. The street was there, but it had never held any houses. In fact, one side of the street was a blank wall, the other a tiny park. 'It just ain't here, miss,' the taxi driver said after they'd been up and down the street twice. He consulted his *A-Z*. 'And there's no other street by that name in London.' She asked him to take her back.

'We just can't get involved,' Matt said over a cup of tea in the residence. 'It may be fishy, but that man left of his own free will. I don't know how he was persuaded to leave, but he was. Who d'you want to tell?'

Who could she tell—and tell them what? She didn't know.

She rang A and E and got the address of where the man had been found. It was the other side of the hospital from where she'd just been. She looked it up in her own *A-Z*, and guessed it wasn't the best of areas.

Now she seemed to be working on some kind of

autopilot, as if she were driven by some force other than her own free will. She went down a floor and borrowed a district nurse's uniform from a friend. It looked well on her and she admired herself in it, thinking it was smarter than her own greens or white coat. It would be easy for her to take a couple of hours off tomorrow afternoon—what she had in mind she could do then.

Next morning she wondered again if she was doing right. Should she confide in someone? She knew Matt wasn't the right one. The only other person would be James. Speedily, she gave up the idea. She had to get James out of her life.

It was easy to arrange. She left the ward at lunchtime, changed into the nurse's uniform and put a blue mac over it. She took another taxi. The driver was surprised at the street name she gave him. 'Not a very nice neighbourhood, miss,' he said.

It was amazing how quickly London could change. In five minutes she travelled from an area of expensive shops and prosperous businesses to this littered, graffitti-scarred wilderness. There were large blocks of flats, with the odd, brave flowerpots on the balconies. Most of the buildings were crumbling Victorian tenements. The few people she saw didn't look at her. She felt like a stranger in her own country.

Too soon she was at her destination. 'Want me to wait for you?' the taxi driver asked. 'This place looks a bit of a dump.'

'I'll be all right. I may be here a while.' She paid him, and the black cab disappeared.

It was a cul-de-sac she walked down, not a residen-

tial street but little more than an alley. There were
rough warehouses, a locked-up garage, a piece of der-
elict land. She got to the street end. The place was
completely deserted. Not a person to be seen.

She thought she would turn back, find her way to
the nearest main road and pick up a taxi to take her
back. As she did so the certainty hit her again, so
strongly that she had to lean against the dirty brick wall
for support. Someone needed her help. Someone was
dying, near, very near her. It had never been like this
before. It wasn't one person—it was more than one.
People were dying!

There was a stout door set back in the nearest warehouse. She climbed to it up three crumbling steps, then
frowned, slightly surprised. A new, expensive-looking
deadlock was set by the side of the old keyhole. She
looked around. There was barbed wire along the top of
every wall, tiny windows with bars across the inside.
She hammered on the door. There was no answer, and
after five minutes she hammered again. She had a feeling of being watched, and she thought she saw a
shadow flit across the darkness behind the nearest window. She hammered a third time. It was almost an anti-
climax when the door was opened.

'Yes?' a tall man asked politely. He was black, but
that wasn't surprising. Most of the people in the neighbourhood were black.

Now she had someone to speak to, Delyth wasn't
quite sure of what to say. She hadn't planned this far
ahead. She stammered, 'Er…two days ago there was a
fight outside here. A man was injured. D'you know
anything about it?'

'I'm afraid not, miss. We do get some violence down here. There is a very troublesome public house down the road.'

'So you can't help me? The man was signed out of my hospital. We think he may be seriously ill.'

'This is only an import-export agency. We bring goods in from my own country. I know of no one who has been ill.'

'I see.' Her shoulders sagged. 'Sorry to have troubled you. It was my mistake.'

'Not at all.' Smiling, the man moved to close the door. He had two gold front teeth. She remembered Matt's description of the person who had signed John out.

Quickly, she said, 'I'll make my report and the police will probably be round later.' She was lying as she'd never lied before, but the man didn't know that.

'Police? I see no need for them. Do come inside. We can discuss it.'

Too late she realised her mistake. 'No, I have to go. I...'

He had detected her suspicions. When she turned he grabbed her, hauled her backwards into the doorway. She tried to wrench herself out of his grasp and grab for the door. But she was unbalanced. She just turned her head sufficiently to see him, not at all polite now, grasping a great lump of wood. It swung at her head and she couldn't duck. There was an explosion of agonising pain and she fell, putting out a hand to save herself. There was another flash of pain in her hand, and then a merciful semi-darkness. She slumped to the floor.

A tiny part of her brain was never quite extinguished. She knew she was on the floor. She felt herself being turned onto her back, dragged away from the doorway by the shoulders. The man was shouting, but she didn't understand him. Then someone else came and picked up her legs, and she was carried, down, down. She didn't know where. It got cooler.

Then there was the creak of another door opening. She was dropped carelessly on a cold floor. Behind her a door slammed to. Her nostrils detected a smell, a medical smell, a smell of illness, but like nothing else she'd smelt before. Then she lost consciousness completely.

She was unconscious for only a minute or so. She awoke to coldness, her head and wrist agonising. She didn't want to open her eyes, she wanted to sleep, but consciousness was rushing back. She felt a twinge of nausea, and took deep breaths to stop herself vomiting—and that made her come awake even faster. Why did her head and hand hurt so much? Somehow she managed to sit upright.

There was a dim light in the room, and by it she could see her right hand. Ugh! An automatic expression of disgust struck her. Two of her fingers were sticking out backwards at a ludicrous angle. They were dislocated. Without thinking, she grasped the two and yanked at them. She felt them click back into place. They hurt—but the pain was endurable. Then she realised there was another pain further back along her arm. Delicately, she tried to move her wrist. The feeling of crepitus—a bony grating—was unmistakable. Her wrist was broken. And she had an evil headache.

She felt her head. A trickle of blood, a great lump. It hurt, and she suspected it was going to hurt more, but she didn't think she was concussed. If I can think about it, and decide that I'm not concussed, then I'm probably not concussed, she told herself. Then she realised that her careful analysis of the situation was just a way of avoiding being afraid. The full horror of her situation broke over her. She had been attacked, imprisoned—goodness knew what might happen to her next. Things like this just didn't happen to people like her!

Nobody knew where she was. Where was she? She wished she had someone with her. She shut her eyes again, her mind filled with the silent screamed message. James! I'm here! Come and get me.

Then she decided that was foolish. She had to look after herself.

She pulled herself slowly to her feet and looked round. She was in a large, dimly lit cellar. There were no windows. The walls were stone and the ceiling low, the door behind her locked.

She wasn't alone. There was a groaning, the sighing and wheezing of breathing. And that smell! It wasn't just unwashed humanity, though that was part of it. There was the smell of illness. At the far side of the room were six truckle beds. She walked over to see who was in them.

On the way she found an open door leading to a lavatory and filthy washbasin. Running water on her hands, she splashed it over her face. Then, a little more alert, she went to inspect the beds.

Six beds with six men in them. All had the same

tribal scars on their faces that John had. She recognised the third man—it was John. The men who were awake looked at her uncomprehendingly. She felt their foreheads—they all had a fever. John hadn't had a fever yesterday. What had brought it on so fast?

One man seemed to be most ill of all. She eased down the sheet covering him, trying not to gag at the smell. There was a rough dressing over his armpit. She peered at the ulcerous patch underneath. Then she turned to the next man and looked under his blanket. Her suspicions were confirmed. He had a large growth on his groin. She'd never come across it before, but she'd seen pictures, read accounts. The growth was a called a bubo. These men were affected by bubonic plague. In the Middle Ages it had been called the Black Death. And it was intensely infectious.

She went to sit on the floor on the far side of the room, and thought. Clear, logical thinking took away some of the terror of her situation. Half-remembered notes came back to her, things she'd thought she'd never have to deal with. The last outbreak in England had been in the 1920s, she thought, and occasional cases since in people coming from abroad. It could be very infectious, if it was airborne, usually carried from human to human by sneezing. Atishoo, Atishoo, all fall down. That was the nursery rhyme, and it referred to the plague. But she hadn't heard anyone sneezing. That was good. Presumably these men had the flea-borne disease, and that was far less infectious.

There was good news. Treatment was easy. Tetracycline or doxycycline would quickly clear it up.

If these men were in hospital they could be certainly cured... Behind her, the door opened.

She turned, in some strange way anger replacing her fear. In the doorway was Goldtooth, behind him an even larger man. She guessed he was the one who had helped carry her.

'These men are ill!' she snapped. 'They need immediate hospital care.'

Goldtooth smiled unpleasantly. 'I'm afraid that's not possible. However, I have food here. You may feed them if you wish.' The man behind him moved into the room and put a large pan of something on the floor.

'I can't treat them here! And if I'm not back soon, my friends will come for me.'

'I rather suspect they would have been here before if they knew where you were. Anyway, that is a chance I am willing to take.'

'These men are here illegally, aren't they?'

He shrugged. 'Workers are needed everywhere. Unfortunately, these seem to have brought their own illness with them.'

She couldn't believe his calmness. 'You know they're going to die if they don't have treatment? Even worse, they could start an epidemic.'

Obviously he didn't want to think about that. His previous good temper disappeared. 'Feed them if you wish,' he snarled. 'I have arrangements to make. This place is no longer any use to us. We'll have to move out.'

'What about me?' She didn't mean to ask the question—it showed fear. But somehow it had slipped out.

'You know nothing. When we go we'll release you.'

She didn't believe him. But the door shut before she could say anything.

The pan contained some kind of mealie porridge. It was warm and presumably nourishing, and she tried to spoon some of it into the mouths of the sick men. They didn't seem very interested so she fetched them water.

The man she thought the most sick moaned. She felt his forehead, took his pulse, listened to his breathing. This man was going to die—soon! She ran to the door, pounded it with her fist, then kicked it. 'There's a man here, dying!' she screamed.

Nothing happened. When she stopped it struck her how silent the place was. No sound of traffic or anything. In London that was *very* unusual. She could die here and no one would know.

She slumped by the door. Suddenly her head hurt. It struck her that since she'd regained consciousness she'd been kept active by adrenaline. She'd seen this kind of hyperactivity in accident victims before. But it soon passed. It was passing for her now. She felt sick. Then she felt tired. If she closed her eyes for a minute, perhaps she'd feel better.

She awoke. Somehow she knew she'd slept for quite some time. Her eyes felt sticky, her body cold and cramped. In front of her the door was opening. She didn't really care. She wasn't even surprised when James was the first man through it.

'Delyth, are you all right?' Even in her confused state she could tell there was a world of pain and anxiety in his voice. He does care a bit about me, she thought as he stooped by her side.

'Just a bump on the head,' she said. 'And I think my wrist is broken.' There was so much she wanted to say to him, but her doctor's training took over. There were things she had to say. 'James, I think these men have bubonic plague. They need—'

'I know what they've got,' he said. 'Relax now. It's all being taken care of.' She looked behind him. The room was filling with men dressed in white overalls and masks. They were bending over her patients. They weren't her patients now—she didn't need to take charge. Throwing her arms around him, she collapsed, weeping, on his shoulder.

For a while he just held her. But then she felt slightly better, and he gave her a quick examination. 'Just your head and wrist? Sure there're no other injuries, nothing broken, no odd pains?'

I was walking around before you came.'

He flicked a torch from his pocket and shone it into her eyes. 'I don't think you're concussed,' he said, 'but we'll see.'

Behind him there was a rattle and two trolleys were wheeled into the room. One stopped by her. 'She seems OK,' James said, and took her shoulders as a paramedic took her thighs.

'There're other people who need attention before...' she started. Then she was gently lifted onto the trolley.

'You're not the doctor now—I am,' James said with some heat. 'I take the decisions. You've done enough. Now you're going to hospital. Delyth, why didn't you tell me what you were doing? I thought we were friends. I thought we could talk. You scared me.' He walked by her side as she was wheeled and carried through the dank corridors of the warehouse. There seemed to be a lot of people here. Policemen, as well as paramedics.

'We are friends,' she mumbled. 'James, you must tell me, how did you know where to find me?'

He squeezed her hand. 'I turned detective. There's been a lot happened you don't know about.'

'But I want to know. I need to—'

'I'll be in to see you later. Just take it easy. You're a patient now, not a doctor.'

He was friendly, but his face gave as little away as ever. Or did it? Was there some pain there, some feeling over and above what she'd expect him to show for a colleague? She thought so. But, then, she knew she'd had a bad blow to the head. Perhaps it was affecting her judgement.

The street outside was busy. As well as ambulances, there were police vehicles and a public health van. There seemed to be an awful lot of people being efficient. She was lifted into an ambulance. 'I'll be in to see you when I can,' James said, 'but for the moment I'm afraid I'm needed here.'

'Come soon,' she said, and closed her eyes.

She wasn't taken to her own hospital. She found herself in a room on her own, with a nurse helping her to undress and wash and lending her a nightie. Then an older doctor came to see her and examined her thoroughly. He carried out all the tests that she would have done, gave her head a CT scan and X-rayed her wrist. 'A nasty bang to the skull,' he told her, 'but I don't think there'll be any lasting consequences. We'll strap up your wrist—it'll stop you working for a while. And

I gather you've been near some rather nasty germs, but I doubt you're infected. However, we'll give you an injection which is certain to stop them getting a grip. Doxycycline, I think. Try to get some sleep.'

So she did try, but a question nagged at her. How had James found her? She thought of her desperate, panic-stricken attempt to send him a message. Had he received it? What a silly idea!

Next morning was odd. She knew she should have been at work, but was quite content just to lie in bed. She wasn't exactly in pain, though her head ached. She felt lethargic. Everything was too much trouble.

With one hand she picked at the breakfast that a nurse brought her. An earnest young doctor came to see her, introducing himself as Dr Myers. With a giggle she realised he was the same as her—a house officer. It was interesting to consider his bedside manner from the patient's point of view. Did he fill her with confidence?

'There's a message for you from the head of your firm,' he told her. 'Dr Forrester. He says you're not to worry about work and he'll be in to see you this afternoon. And a Dr Owen will be in some time this morning.'

Her heart thudded for some reason which she didn't think was to do with her condition.

Dr Myers went on, 'I'm doing my medical house job now, of course, but I'd like to do surgical with Dr Forrester's firm next. Is there any chance of getting onto it, d'you think?'

'You'll learn a lot,' she told him. 'You say this is a medical firm?'

'And how! You've caused all sorts of excitement. The men you came in with are in a ward below. We've never come across anything like this before.'

'It is bubonic plague, isn't it?' she asked. 'How are they all doing?'

He frowned, obviously not wanting to break patient confidentiality.

'Look,' she said, 'I've met them. I even tried to treat them. If you like, they're my patients too.'

That decided him. 'I'm afraid one died last night. But we're pumping doxycycline into the others—they should be all right. We think we've caught them in time. It's an easy disease to treat if you catch it in its early stages.'

After that she just lay there till James came at mid-morning. Normally she would have felt excitement at seeing him, and eagerness to know exactly what had happened, but there was still this feeling of lethargy.

He looked well. Obviously he'd been somewhere where he'd needed to command attention. He wore a dark suit, white silk shirt, college tie. 'Who's trying to look important, then?' she asked feebly.

He leaned over to kiss her on the cheek, then sat by the bed. 'I've been meeting important people,' he told her. 'Medical people, public health people, police, even the Home Office. You've really stirred things up, haven't you?'

'Tell me. I still don't know really what happened.'

'Right. First of all, I've tried to keep you out of

things. I take it the last thing you want is publicity. You don't want to appear in court, do you?'

'No! I couldn't stand it! What would my family think?'

'They might think they had a truly exceptional daughter and sister. But that's by the way. You had a patient injured in a fight. You weren't to know that he was also in the early stages of bubonic plague. The blood you took was tested for blood gases, not anything infectious. Anyway, the patient was an illegal immigrant, smuggled in by our friend with the gold teeth. He got fed up with being confined in a cellar and tried to escape. That's when he was beaten up. Goldteeth found out which hospital he was in and came to the ward and told him that if he didn't come back to the warehouse, he'd be deported as an illegal immigrant. So, with help, he signed himself out. Then the plague got him, as it had his friends. They must have been infected in their own country. Goldteeth just didn't know what to do. He's now co-operating completely with the police. They've got enough on him to lock him up for quite a stretch, without charging him with assault.'

It was a simple but sad story. But there was more she needed to know. 'How did you find me?' she asked.

He showed a touch of anger. 'It was pure chance, Delyth. These people can be desperate…violent. I just came onto the ward and you weren't there. I was a bit surprised so I asked Matt where you were. He said you'd wanted an afternoon off for some reason. When I pressed him he thought you were concerned about a patient that had signed himself out. So I looked for the patient's notes and discovered you'd been in touch with A and E about him. Then Matt told me he'd seen you borrowing a nurse's uniform. I was getting worried.

'I found that you'd sent a blood sample for blood gases, and asked them for the fullest survey—for some reason I asked about diseases. When plague turned up in the results I informed Public Health and the police. They took it from there. It'll be a reasonably happy ending all round. The building will be fumigated, the men treated. Simple, really.'

She tried to concentrate. It wasn't simple, really. 'When do I get out of here?' she asked.

'Ah. You can't really go straight back on the ward. That head of yours isn't so good, and after the traumatic afternoon you had Mr Forrester thinks you ought to have some time off. A month, he thinks. And he's talking about counselling.'

'I don't need counselling! There's nothing wrong— Ow!' She tried to jerk forward. There definitely *was* something wrong with her head.

'When he was told that you were a house officer, the consultant in charge here thought a month off a good idea. So do I and, most important, so does Forrester. His decision, but I agree with it.'

'All right,' she said.

'I'm glad you're being reasonable. I'm going to France for a fortnight next week, and I wouldn't want to have to worry about you while I was away.'

'Very thoughtful of you,' she muttered. Why was he going to France? But there was still something else that was bothering her.

'All this trouble you went to,' she said, 'just because I wasn't on the ward. Why didn't you wait till I was obviously missing? I might have been shopping or something simple like that.'

He shrugged. 'It didn't feel like you. I knew something was wrong.'

She seized on his confession. 'You *knew* something was wrong. Matt wasn't worried, was he? Why should you be?'

'It was a good thing I did get worried,' he pointed out, slightly irritated.

'It was in the early afternoon, wasn't it?' She could tell the conversation was making him uncomfortable, but she didn't intend to relent.

'Yes, I think so. You weren't on the ward and I thought it odd.'

'James, when I was thrown into that cellar and I first came to, I was terrified. I didn't know what to do. So I thought of you, harder than I've ever thought of anything in my life before. I wanted you with me. It was early afternoon. And that's when you first worried about me.'

He smiled at her gently—which infuriated her. 'Your sixth sense again, Delyth. It was nothing like that. I was just concerned about a colleague. I would have done the same for anyone.'

'Are you sure about that?'

His answer was bland. 'I'm certain,' he said.

CHAPTER EIGHT

JAMES knew it was a tricky manoeuvre for a house officer to perform. Insertion of a central line into the jugular vein involved locating the needle and then the cannula just to the side of the carotid artery.

Carefully, Matt felt the pulse of the great neck artery with his left hand, then slid home the needle with his other hand, at an angle of 45 degrees. He was successful in finding the vein. Blood appeared in his syringe. As James watched, Matt withdrew his needle and then re-inserted a larger-bore needle. All was going according to plan. The next step was to introduce the guide wire. Matt slid the soft end first down the hollow needle, and carefully fed the wire into the vein. When about half of the wire was in the vein he removed the needle, nicked the skin at the entry point and threaded the dilator onto the wire. Then it was only a case of removing the dilator, threading on the cannula, making sure it was sterile and securing it.

'That was very good, Matt,' James said when they had looked at a chest X-ray and seen that the cannula was properly in place. 'I'll watch the next time you do it, but after that you'll be on your own. Remember, if you should accidentally hit the carotid artery—and one day you will—apply full pressure for five minutes.'

Their patient needed TNP—total parenteral nutrition. Because it was impossible for the man to take in sufficient food by mouth, it was being introduced straight into the bloodstream—in the heart. They had just fed a tube into the vein.

They walked back to the doctors' room for coffee. The normally high-spirited Matt seemed unusually quiet. James wondered what was wrong.

'I gather you've been to see Delyth,' Matt said after an uncomfortable silence.

'Yes, I have. She looks well, but I agree that she shouldn't return to work for a while.'

There was another pause, then Matt said, 'I wonder if I could have a word with you some time?'

'I'm always ready to help, Matt. I've got a few minutes now.'

Matt looked even more uncomfortable. 'It's not anything medical. It's something personal. Could we meet outside the hospital?'

Warily James said, 'We could if you wish. It's about Delyth, isn't it?'

'Yes, sir,' Matt said defiantly.

'Well, how about the Clubroom tonight? We could meet a bit earlier than usual—say about nine?'

'Thank you, that'd be fine, sir. Now I'd better get on.'

James watched him walk out of the room, his coffee untouched. Matt had returned to formality, even though James had told him that he was very happy to be addressed by his first name—except when they were in front of a patient together. James thought he knew what Matt was going to say. Now he had time to think about what he was going to answer. What was he going to answer?

James hadn't been to the Clubroom for a while, not since he'd stopped meeting Delyth there. He arrived early, wanting to sit, have a drink and collect his thoughts before Matt came. When he walked into the room he felt a sudden jolt of disappointment. There would be no Delyth to meet him. He hadn't realised how much he missed those shared late evenings. Still, he reminded himself morosely, it had been his own decision. Why wasn't he happy with it?

He bought himself a beer, and got one for Matt, too. He thought that Matt was going to ask him about his feelings for Delyth, and he still didn't know what he was going to say. All afternoon he had pondered—and got nowhere. It struck him that Delyth had affected him much, much more than any of the women with whom he'd had brief and inconclusive affairs. Perhaps he was wrong about his feelings for her? He shrugged angrily. That idea was ridiculous! He knew what he wanted.

Matt came into the room, looking both uncomfortable and determined. James remembered when he, too, had been in love. Not once but twice. For a moment he remembered the excitement, the exhilaration, the way love had coloured everything he'd done. Life had been brighter then. Then he remembered the unutterable sense of loss afterwards. He wasn't going through that pain again.

Matt walked over to his table. 'I got you a beer,' James said. 'Sit down and we'll talk about how you're in love with Delyth and you don't know what her feelings are towards you.'

Matt looked amazed. 'You know?' he asked.

'I'm not unobservant,' James said gently. 'I know you think a lot of her.'

Matt took a chair and drank from his beer. 'She started as a friend,' he said. 'In fact, she still is a friend. It's just that…I feel bad that I paid no attention to her fears about the missing patient. She tried to confide in me, but I paid no attention. Then you spotted something was wrong and you found her.'

'It was sheer chance,' James assured him. Then he drank some of his own beer and frowned. Why *had* he been so upset? Why had he gone to so much trouble? It so happened that he had been completely right—but he might not have been. The word 'intuition' crossed his mind but he rejected it. Absolute rubbish!

'Anyway,' Matt said, 'I want to thank you. She is… That is, I want her to be…more than a friend now.'

'So you've come to warn me off her?' James asked flatly.

The stark question upset Matt. James saw the blood rise in his cheeks. 'Yes, I have,' Matt said. 'I think that for a senior member of hospital staff to take advantage of a junior member is…despicable.'

James felt the rage rising within him. How dared this young fool interfere with…? Did he think he was the only person in the world to have feelings? But fortunately he managed to keep calm. After a silence he said, 'It must have taken quite a lot of nerve to say that.'

It wasn't the answer the now pale Matt was expecting. 'It did,' he admitted.

Neither spoke for a while. Then James said, 'I'm not going to talk about my relationship with Delyth. She

may talk to you if she wishes.' With a secret ironic
smile he remembered that he had held back when he'd
found that Delyth was a virgin. What would Matt think
of that? Not, of course, that he intended to tell him.

He went on, 'I'll just tell you that I have as high an
opinion of her as you have. And I would never take
advantage of my senior position. Like you, I think it's
despicable.'

Eagerly Matt asked, 'Then you're not interested in
her—that way, I mean?'

James drained his glass. He looked at Matt's barely
touched beer and said with a grin, 'Your round, isn't
it?'

Matt smiled tightly. 'I'll fetch you a beer,' he said.
'It'll give you time to think of your answer.'

James winced as Matt walked over to the bar. One
day this young man would be a good doctor. He had
the right feeling for people. When he returned James
said, 'I told you I wouldn't talk about my relationship
with Delyth—that's up to her. I'll just use one quaint,
stupid, old-fashioned word. With her my behaviour will
be honourable. D'you believe me?'

'Yes,' said Matt after a pause. There was another
silence and then he went on, 'I hope I'll be like you
when I get older.'

'How's that?' asked James, genuinely curious.

'Clever,' said Matt.

'I don't think I really like being a patient,' Delyth said.

She felt at a disadvantage, looking up at Michael
Forrester, the consultant who was head of her firm.
Usually they stood side by side, either in white coats,

looking down at a patient in bed, or in theatre greens. Now he was elegant in a grey pinstripe three-piece suit and she was in a floral nightie. It just wasn't right.

'I can understand that,' he replied urbanely, 'but perhaps it's good for all of us to see things from the other side, as it were.'

She wondered how long it had been since he'd been made to lie in bed when he'd known there was nothing wrong with him, but she wisely said nothing.

'I'm pleased to see you making such good progress, such a rapid recovery,' he added.

This was her chance. 'I feel much better now,' she rushed in, 'and I'd really like to start work on the ward again soon. I know my wrist will make things difficult but I could do some things. I'm sorry if I acted a bit precipitately but—'

He raised his hand to stop her. 'What you did was in some ways admirable.' He fetched a chair to sit beside her. Unhappily, she realised she was in for a long talk. Consultants didn't normally sit in chairs by bedsides.

'I've been making a few enquiries about you,' he went on when he had made himself comfortable. 'With the pressure of work, too often we don't know enough about the young doctors who come onto our wards. Perhaps we should. I've been told that you worked extremely hard for your degree—as most medical students do. But after the exams most of them took a much-needed holiday. You didn't. Instead, you worked long hours at a cottage hospital near your home, with your local GP—a Dr Alun Roberts.'

That was true. 'He encouraged me to apply for medical school,' she explained. 'And he helped me in the course. When I got the chance to do something for him—'

'So you didn't have a holiday,' he interrupted. 'Delyth, I don't know what people have been saying to you. But one thing must be emphasised. You made a serious error of judgement. As it happens, the consequences haven't been too bad. They could have been disastrous. The least you should have done was tell people what you were thinking of. Isn't it hammered into you when you first get on a ward? Everything is written down. You make certain that other people know what you are doing.'

'I suppose so,' she mumbled.

He put a crumpled envelope on the table by her bed, and motioned for her to open it. Out of it dropped ten pound coins.

'A patient called Birdie Jones came to my clinic yesterday,' he said. 'He asked especially to see you. When I said you weren't available, he asked me to give you this. In time I got him to tell me why.'

'It was my money. I can do what I like with it,' she pointed out resentfully.

'True. And I must say I took to young Birdie. But what I'm saying is that as doctors we must be caring and compassionate—the patient is always a human being, not a case. But you cannot interfere too much with patients' lives. Our job is a medical one. That is all we have time for. I think you're in danger of getting too close, even too involved, and I think it's dangerous. You're overtired. So I'm prescribing rest for another three weeks. Is that all right?'

'I suppose so,' she mumbled. She knew she didn't have much choice.

'Good. Now, we can take it that you don't have plague. It's an unpleasant disease, but laughably easy to treat if caught early enough. Your head and wrist are coming along reasonably well. I know you could go home—I've heard about your family from Dr Owen. But I've got another idea. My brother has a farmhouse in the south of France which he's converted so that people can stay there. A lot of medical staff go there—we have a relationship with a hospital nearby. In fact, Dr Owen is going there next weekend for a fortnight. He's going to work. I want you to go with him and rest.'

She looked up, bewildered. 'Have you asked him?' she asked.

'No, but I'm sure he'd be only too pleased to take you with him. Someone for him to talk to on the journey.'

It struck her that perhaps Mr Forrester had been right. He should know a little more about the young doctors who came onto his ward. Then he wouldn't have suggested this.

'I think a fortnight in a warmer climate will be good for you,' he went on. 'And let me make one thing clear. You're not coming back onto my firm until I think you're ready.'

'I'd love to go,' she said, 'if you're sure Dr Owen wouldn't mind taking me.'

She wondered why she was so keen to go. Hadn't James made it clear that there was no future for them together?

* * *

Without Delyth the ward's paperwork was piling up. That afternoon Matt was sitting in the doctors' room, patiently working his way through the usual mass of forms. They had to be done so he was doing them. But they were tedious!

James had called in for the notes on a patient he was due to operate on the next day. He saw Matt gloomily at work, and offered to help for half an hour. The two worked together in companionable silence.

The door opened and Mr Forrester peered inside. 'Just been to see Delyth,' he said. 'She's making excellent progress. I've made a couple of phone calls and we've got a replacement for her for the next two weeks. James, I know you're driving down to Villeneuf next Sunday. I thought it a good idea if Delyth went as well to recuperate. You don't mind taking her, do you?'

After a moment's thought James said, 'If she's agreeable. I've hired a big car.'

'That's settled, then.' The consultant left.

James looked at Matt and shrugged. 'Not my idea,' he said.

'I know. You can bring me a bottle of wine back.'

Megan had returned to London by train after a week at home. Her first trip out was to visit her injured sister.

'So I'm going to France with him,' Delyth told Megan. 'D'you think that's a good idea?'

She wriggled inside her dressing-gown. She was getting tired of sitting around, doing nothing. She'd tried to write a letter home, but had given up. Between them, she and Megan had decided that she wouldn't tell their parents about what had happened. They would only have worried. And it was hard to write a letter home without mentioning that she was in hospital herself.

'I'm not sure going away with James Owen is a good idea,' Megan said. 'Though the stay in France sounds fine.'

'He won't be…pushy or anything like that.'

'I know,' Megan said sharply. 'I can tell from his face. That's the least of my worries. It's not his actions I'm worried about, it's your feelings. You've never been like this before. I think you're pushing yourself into a situation that'll hurt you. And I don't know why. Anyway, what about this young doctor you were seeing?'

Delyth sighed. She didn't feel happy about the way she had treated Matt, though she had tried to make her feelings clear to him.

'He came to see me, and he was ever so sweet. But I realised that I was just using him to try and forget James. It wasn't fair on him. So I told him that I liked him a lot and hoped we'd still be friends, but that would be all.'

'I'll bet he loved that. What did he say?'

'He was upset, but he took it very well. Said I'd had a nasty shock…needed to recuperate…this wasn't the time to make decisions. We could talk when I was fully better and certainly he wouldn't force himself on me.'

'Sounds a good sort,' announced Megan, chewing on one of the grapes she'd brought. 'Are you sure you want to get rid of him?'

'I wish he'd got angry,' Delyth confessed. 'He was entitled to, and I could have dealt with that better. I found myself liking and admiring him even more.'

'But not loving him?'

'No, not loving him.'

Megan scowled, then stood and limped over to help herself to more grapes. 'I thought I'd got you settled,' she said accusingly. 'Now you've changed your mind and I have to carry on worrying. You said you knew James wasn't for you. You were going to give him up and remain friends. Fine, I thought, very civilised, very sensible. He'd made his position clear—he couldn't have been more obvious. But now you're thinking there's some hope for you after all. I'm right, aren't I?'

'Well, perhaps I am just a bit,' Delyth admitted.

'Why? I know he drove me home but, other than that, has he given you any reason to think that he wants a lasting relationship with you? Is it just because he rode in to save you from danger, like some knight on a big white horse?'

'He thinks of me as a friend and a colleague,' Delyth cried. 'He likes me.'

'And that's all. But you know better than him what he's thinking.'

Delyth remembered her terrified silent plea when she'd been locked in the cellar. He had responded to that. No one else had worried—only James had heard her and come to seek her out.

'I don't know what he wants,' she said. 'He's had a hard life. I know there's a black side to his soul but I think he might improve.'

Megan shook her head despairingly. 'Six sisters are artists. And the single scientist amongst us is the one refusing to listen to logic. Delyth, you worry me! You're throwing yourself at this man! He's told you he wouldn't mind being your lover—something temporary. He's made that very clear. You can't blame him if he takes advantage of what you're offering him.'

' I'm not offering him anything,' Delyth said. 'We're just travelling to France together and we should enjoy each other's company on the way. That's all, Anyway, wouldn't you like James as a brother-in-law?'

'I give up,' Megan said.

But when James came to see Delyth again she was much more uncertain. Perhaps Megan was right. Perhaps she was making a serious error of judgement. James was friendly, but nothing more. On Saturday she was to return to the residence by taxi, pack, then get to bed early. 'Remember how tiring a few days in bed can be,' he told her. 'You're not going to be half as strong as you think.'

'I just want to get out of this ward. Doing nothing is driving me mad.'

'You'll be doing something on Sunday,' he told her drily. 'I want you up at half past four in the morning. We're catching the ferry from Portsmouth at half past seven.'

'I've never had any problem getting out of bed.'

'D'you know what clothes to take? It'll be warmer than England, but we're going to Aquitaine, which means the watery district, so it can pour down.'

'I've been reading this book about the area. I know what to take. James, I'm really looking forward to this. And, let's be clear, I want to pay my way. I'm not going to—'

'It's all been taken care of,' he told her. 'But you'll

need to spend something when you're there. If you give me a cheque for a hundred pounds I'll get you some francs and arrange some traveller's cheques. Anything else I can get for you?'

As in everything he did, he was efficient and thoughtful. But he wasn't loving. He treated her like any friend and she felt a tiny bit hurt. But they were going to be so much together. Perhaps love between them would suddenly develop. If it didn't...her future looked bleak.

Even though James had warned her, she was surprised at how weak she had become. She shouldn't have been surprised. She remembered big, strong men who couldn't believe how powerless they were after two or three weeks' bed rest. She now had a fresh, lighter dressing on her wrist. It was still uncomfortable but she could do most things with it.

Matt came in a taxi to fetch her. She felt grateful, and slightly tearful at this. But he was nothing but friendly and concerned. There were no reproaches. He helped her to her room, fetched her the inevitable mug of tea and went to find her cases from the store down the corridor.

'You'll want a bit of time to yourself,' he said. 'You'll need to rest after packing. But you know my room—shout if there's anything at all I can do.'

'Thanks, Matt, you're a real friend.'

Packing didn't take long. There were few decisions—she'd carefully made a list while lying in bed. Then she discovered Matt had been right. She did want

time to herself. She wasn't interested in gossip about
the ward or work. She decided to lie on her bed.

For a moment there was a quick feeling of panic.
This was just not like her. She felt remote, detached,
not concerned with things she knew should concern
her. She wondered about her parents. Megan had said
that she would write to them, saying that Delyth was
very busy and had been offered the chance to observe
in a hospital in France. This was almost true. But
Delyth didn't feel the guilt she would have expected at
half deceiving them.

Still in her dreamlike state, she checked her packing,
looked at the medication she'd been left, set the alarm
and decided to sleep. She knew she'd have no difficulty
waking as she was accustomed to early rising.

It was still dark at half past four. She showered,
dressed in the tracksuit that James had suggested,
packed her nightie, washbag and other things in the
little bag he had told her she was to take on board.
Then she waited till he knocked softly on the door. He
had insisted that she didn't try to carry her cases down.

She thrilled to see him. Like her he was dressed for
comfort, in cords and a loose sweater. She felt they
were to share an adventure, at the beginning of something that might be more than a mere journey. For a
second, as he first looked at her, she thought that he
felt the same way. But perhaps it was just a friendly
smile.

They went downstairs to his hired car, a burgundy-
coloured Discovery, a bit smaller and more modern
than Megan's great vehicle. In the back was a pile of

papers and equipment he was taking to the French hospital. He helped her up onto her seat.

The London traffic was very quiet at this time of the morning. They threaded their way easily through the centre and were soon on the M 3 at a steady seventy miles an hour. She didn't sleep, as she had done the last time he'd driven her. She wanted to experience every moment of the day.

There weren't too many cars driving their way, but the oncoming vehicles were now in one long procession. 'Commuters,' he told her. 'Coming in for their daily boring work. Isn't it exciting to be escaping, going the other way?'

He'd caught her mood exactly. 'It's like when we used to drive off on our holidays together,' she told him. 'It's starting a journey, watching the world come to life as dawn breaks. It's magic.'

They didn't talk much after that, being content to sit quietly. Instead he fumbled in his pocket and clicked in a tape. The soft voice of Lena Horne filled the car, singing love songs.

'That's one of my favourites,' she told him. 'We have tastes in common.'

He smiled gently. 'I do like it,' he said. 'But I must confess I phoned Megan and asked her what music you liked. I bought this tape specially for you.'

'I see,' she said. She wondered what to make of that.

The morning was grey at first, but then the sun made a weak appearance. Eventually they swung off the motorway and onto the coast road, and then parked in the queue for the ferry at Portsmouth. Now she *did* feel she was going on holiday.

Ahead of them were two giant white ships, impossibly high. There was the screaming of gulls. They were directed expertly from queue to queue, then up a rattling steel ramp to the hold. There was the glimpse of water far below, and then they were packed in tightly with the other cars. Carefully, they climbed out.

As Delyth wriggled past the other cars, at James's suggestion carrying a coat and her little bag, it struck her that she hadn't left so many arrangements to another person since she was a little child. Why had she so much faith in James's decisions? It seemed as if she knew that everything he wanted she would want, too.

'Travelling excites me,' he told her, and she knew it. She could tell by the eagerness of his step and the brightness of his eye. 'We're six hours on this ship. I thought you might like to stay on deck as we sail, have a quick breakfast and then sleep.'

'Whatever you think,' she assured him. 'It sounds wonderful to me.' There were quite a few sets of stairs until they got to where they could be in the open air. Her legs were weak and he had to help her.

'When we get to Villeneuf I'll give you a set of graded exercises,' he told her. 'After a fortnight you'll be as good as new. Just don't try to do too much.'

'No, Doctor,' she said with mock humility, and he turned and grinned at her.

The great ship hummed. They saw the water boiling far below them as slowly and gracefully they backed out of their berth and set off down the Solent. Delyth decided she had been too long in hospital, and was eager for new sights. They stood silently together, watching the grey sleekness of a destroyer, the vastness of an aircraft carrier, the amazing rigging of Nelson's *Victory*. They smelled the sea, listened again to the screaming of the gulls. Then they passed a tiny fort in the water and they were out on the open sea.

'Fancy some breakfast?' James asked, and she realised she was indeed hungry. When she moved away from the rail she staggered a little, and instantly his arm was around her. It was only for support, and for a moment she leaned against him. It was very comforting.

Then she moved away. It was good of him to offer her this lift. She wouldn't repay his kindness by showing herself to be expecting a relationship that he didn't want. But if he *did* find that he wanted it...

In the café he found her a table by the window and fetched them both a breakfast tray. She wasn't hungry—she was ravenous. Usually she had a good appetite, but had reacted to life as a hospital patient by eating less than usual. Now, after the sea air, she tucked into the cereal, bacon and egg that he had brought her. It was so satisfying. And then...

'You're tired,' he told her. He was right—she was exhausted. But she wasn't going to admit it.

'I am not tired,' she told him, then contradicted herself by yawning hugely.

'Don't worry, I've got everything planned. Come on down to our cabin.'

'Our cabin?' she asked. This was interesting.

'Your cabin, then. For every double ticket there's a cabin. You're lucky, yours is an outside one.'

She followed him down more stairs and along long corridors. The humming of the ship's engines grew louder. Now she knew she was tired. The prospect of bed was inviting. Eventually he checked the number on a door and opened it to show her into a tiny cabin.

There were two berths, one on top of the other. There was a ladder and a place to hang coats. Another door opened into an equally tiny shower room. It all seemed wonderfully cosy.

'Bed,' he suggested. 'I'll give you a knock three quarters of an hour before we dock. That'll give you time for a shower and a sandwich.'

She frowned. 'What about you? You need your sleep too.'

'I'll catch a couple of hours in a reclining chair. They're very comfortable. I'm a doctor, I can sleep anywhere.'

'No.' She was firm. 'We're colleagues. You can have the top bunk. I'll be unhappy if you don't. Besides, you've got a long way to drive and you shouldn't be tired. You've got a precious cargo. Me.'

He looked down at her sitting on the lower bunk. 'Yes,' he agreed, 'I have a precious cargo. OK, you go to bed and I promise to come back in an hour or so.'

'Take the key,' she told him.

When he'd gone she changed into her nightie and slipped between the cool sheets. The engine's hum was hypnotic. She had intended to think about a few things but instead, she slept at once.

She awoke to the smell of coffee. James was offering her a plastic cup. 'We'll be there soon,' he said. 'Drink this and then have a shower.'

She blinked. 'Have I been asleep all this time?'

'Sleeping like a baby. I came in after an hour and

tiptoed round, but I don't think a full force gale would have woken you. So I also slept.'

Delyth took the coffee, noticing that his hair was wet. 'I've just had a shower myself,' he told her. 'Now, I'll leave you for twenty minutes and then we'll watch the ship dock.'

After the shower she felt refreshed, full of excitement, eager for the next part of the journey. He collected her and they had a swift sandwich in the cafeteria, then just had time to watch the ferry slide neatly into what seemed an impossibly small space. There was the reverse scramble to get in the car, the wait which now seemed longer and then the clanking out into daylight.

They were in France! She saw signs telling them to drive on the right, and they followed other, largely British cars. The houses seemed different, the fields looked different, even the weather felt different. She glanced at him, driving confidently, and saw that he, too, was enjoying himself. 'Landfall,' he told her. 'The start of something new. Always exciting, isn't it?'

'Yes,' she agreed, 'an exciting start of something new.'

Their route took them across Normandy to the *autoroute* at Tours. From there they would curve down across the west of France. For the first stage of the journey they were both content to watch and say little. After they'd joined the *autoroute* he drove for about thirty miles and then stopped.

'I don't believe in driving for too long,' he told her. 'We'll stretch our legs, have a drink.' He took her for a walk around. French motorway stops were superior to English ones, she thought. Not as busy, better landscaped and somehow different. She enjoyed herself, and when they started the drive again she was invigorated. She wanted something new now.

He handed her a bag. 'Pick a tape,' he urged her. 'Music for gentle driving.'

'No. If you don't mind, I'd rather talk to you.'

'Talk about anything you like,' he invited. 'I'm a good listener.'

'I know you are. You're a good talker, too, but recently you've been gentle with me. You've not wanted to push me too hard because of the injury to my head. True?'

He was silent a moment and then said, 'Yes, that's true, Delyth.'

'Well, I'm now declaring myself officially well. There are a couple of things I want to ask you, and I also want to tell you something.' She paused. 'You know I've made a statement to the police about what happened in the warehouse?'

'Yes. In fact, I've seen some of it.'

'Good. Apart from that, everyone has been tiptoeing round me, not wanting to ask questions in case I was upset. Even the policewoman was extra nice to me. I felt like an invalid. I was even offered counselling!'

'You should have accepted,' he told her. 'There are people who haven't been able to get back to work after suffering what you did.'

'Well, I'm tougher than them. And now I want to talk about what happened.'

For a moment he took his eyes off the road to glance at her. 'Are you sure that's a good idea?'

'It's an excellent idea. And it's you that's going to be cross-examined, not me. I've asked you about it once. Now I want more details.' She took a breath. 'We've established that I did something stupid chasing after that man, especially not telling anyone what I was doing. When I was gone Matt, who cares for me a lot, didn't worry at all. Why should he? But you did. Why should you, a very busy doctor, suddenly decide that I might be in danger, go to quite considerable trouble to find out where I'd gone, even contact the police? On the face of it, it doesn't seem necessary.'

'It was necessary,' he pointed out, 'and the more I enquired the more certain I became.'

'But why did you worry in the first place?'

He laughed. 'I know where you're going, Delyth. You think this sixth sense of yours contacted me. I thought it only told you when people were ill.'

She ignored his laughter. She thought it sounded slightly forced. 'That's true,' she said. 'But I was terrified, more than I've ever been in my life before. So I lay there and I tried to talk to you. And after I tried I felt better, and when you turned up in the cellar I wasn't really surprised.'

He took a hand off the wheel and laid it on hers. 'Yours is one account,' he said. 'Another is that, as you said, you were terrified. You were disorientated, not capable of rational thought. In that state the mind seizes any comfort. Sorry, Delyth, that's all there is to it.'

'Possibly,' she said. 'What about your actions, then?'

He shrugged. 'Matt didn't worry because he'd just seen you. I came along and realised your actions were a bit unusual. And quickly I found out enough to be very suspicious.'

She had to admit that what he said was plausible. She wondered if it was true.

They drove on without speaking further. Now they were well into France she thought there was a difference in the weather, even in the quality of the light. She was enjoying herself, but he misjudged her silence.

'I'm sorry to doubt your theories,' he said, 'but I've always been a rationalist. Still, we're good friends and I think we can agree to differ. Tell me what else you wanted to talk about. I'll talk about anything.'

'D'you mean that?'

'Any subject at all.'

'Then I want you to tell me about the two girls you fell in love with.' Delyth looked at him, and saw his face seem to turn to stone. 'Please,' she hurried on, 'don't talk if you don't want to. I don't want to pry.'

After a silence he said, 'Nobody has ever tried to talk to me about either of them. I mean really talk. I don't know if I can.'

'Talking can be good. Aren't you the man who's in favour of counselling?'

She saw a tiny smile. 'You're a tough one to fight with,' he said. 'Do you talk? Do you talk about me?'

'To a certain extent. I talk to Megan most, even though we're not at all alike. She likes you a lot.'

'I'll bet that's not all.'

'No,' she said cautiously. 'She says there's something in your face that's hidden. She thinks you might hurt me, even though you don't want to.'

'Do you think I might hurt you?'

'I think you could,' she said simply. 'I know there's a black side to you. But that night when you...when we nearly...I was very upset at the time. But afterwards I thought a lot of you because of it.'

'It wasn't one of the best nights of my life,' he growled.

He had been slowing down, now he turned into an *aire de repos*. She'd noticed these and thought they were a really good idea. They weren't proper motorway service stations. There were no shops or petrol pumps. Just a tiny park. There was a toilet block, a landscaped area, rustic tables in the shade. She'd seen people picnicking at them. Now James parked. 'We'll have a little rest,' he said.

She followed him as he walked up a bank and rounded a clump of trees. In a little hollow was a table. They sat opposite each other. Behind them was a vast green field, the spire of a church beyond that. The hum of traffic was muted, and they seemed entirely alone.

He put his elbows on the table, then reached over and took her clasped hands, holding them loosely between his.

'Erin and then Hilary,' he said.

'With Erin, we were together so long that we didn't realise what was happening to us. Love grew slowly. We had so much else to think about at work. We had such a lot in common, suffering through the last two years of medical school and finals. Then we were both doctors. The world was in front of us. We had wild plans for when we finished our house officers' jobs. Our love for each other was part of everything we did. And she died. You've no idea what it's like—to wake up morning after morning, expecting to find a head on the pillow beside you and it's not there. No idea what it's like to think you're clawing your way out of a nightmare, and then to wake to find it's true.'

The terrible thing was his voice. There was no trace of emotion, no indication of the torment he must have felt—must be still feeling. He spoke softly, reflectively, as if these things had happened to someone else. 'And Hilary?' she prompted.

'That was different to start with. She was a bit older than me, had been hurt in a previous relationship. We were both wary. But things grew. I found myself relaxing, thinking that I could be happy again. And in time I was happy—we both were. But we were content with what we had. We didn't make any plans.'

He paused, and she thought he didn't want to go on. But then he said, 'I remember once, when I was delivering a baby, talking to the mother. It was her second child. The first was happy and loved, this second one was planned and all was going well. But she told me, before we gave her an epidural, that with the pangs of the second baby all the memories of pain from the first birth came flooding back. It was like that when Hilary was knocked down. I'd forgotten the pain of loss. It came flooding back. But I knew there'd be no end to it, no baby for me. She was bound to die.'

She tried in vain to imagine how he must have felt—

the pain, the sheer horror. 'How did you manage?' she asked. 'How did you just…carry on?'

'It wasn't easy. I ran, sometimes twice a day. Exhausting myself, pushing myself to the limit physically. It helped. Running still helps me cope with things.'

Delyth wrestled with wildly different emotions. First there was an overwhelming pity for him. Why should such a good man have to suffer so much agony? And then there was a deep feeling of frustration. He was wrong! She asked, 'So you're not going to fall in love again?'

He didn't reply with the same assurance as he had in the past. He frowned, as if he were hearing the words he was using for the first time, as if he were convincing himself as well as her. 'Why should I, Delyth? I have a happy, fulfilling life. From time to time I meet girls who like my company but don't want commitment. I won't hurt anybody. I would say it's a pretty useful arrangement, wouldn't you?'

'If it makes you happy,' she agreed. 'Are you trying to persuade me or yourself?'

He laughed, a little uneasily. 'You're too shrewd.' His voice altered, and he reached over to touch her cheek. 'But if I ever did want another long-term commitment, Delyth, it would be with someone like you.'

'I suppose that's a start.'

Did he know how deliriously happy he'd just made her?

CHAPTER NINE

THEY decided not to stop at a hotel. Delyth knew James was happy driving, and she urged him to press on. He stopped to make a quick telephone call to say they'd arrive late. Then he reclined her seat, and she dozed as they passed through the sea of great lights that was Bordeaux. Then it was into the dark along another *autoroute*.

It started to rain. 'This is Aquitaine,' he told her. 'What d'you expect?' She rather liked the way the rain rattled on the roof, and once or twice the interior of the car was lit by white sheet lightning. There was the distant rumble of thunder. James drove more slowly on the wet roads.

Then the rain stopped, and they turned off the *autoroute*, drove through a large village and into the darkness again. Only occasional lights on the distant hills showed any sign of civilisation. They turned onto a yet smaller road, and he stopped to read instructions by the navigation light. By now she was very tired, and she wondered how he felt. He looked as if he'd be happy enough to go on for ever!

Then he turned the wheel, the car lurched and there was the crunch of gravel. He stopped. 'We've arrived,' he said.

Exhausted, she stumbled out of the car, helped by an unseen hand. She was led inside what was called

the barn. She had a vague impression of size, of old
beams, old furniture. She sat at a great table. A kindly
couple, Val and Tom, greeted her and gave her a sandwich and a cup of cocoa. They were her host and hostess. Tom looked like his brother Michael Forrester.

James sat opposite her. She wondered how he had
driven so long without showing fatigue. Apart from
little lines round his eyes he looked as fresh as he had
that morning. He smiled at her. 'You're tired,' he said,
stating the obvious.

Her cases were fetched and she was led to a tiny
bedroom and shown the bathroom next door. What if
she had slept on the journey? She would sleep some
more. Within a minute she was in bed—a double, she
noticed. Within two minutes she was asleep.

Next morning was different. She awoke refreshed,
excited even. This stay was going to be some kind of
an adventure. The memory of her fatigue the day before suggested to her that she wasn't as strong as she
used to be, but she'd improve. She had a fortnight—
living next to James.

It was warmer than England. The sun shone through
red checked curtains. She looked around her room and
saw simple pine furniture, her case opened and abandoned on a stool. There was a door into the barn
proper, French windows opening to the sun.

There was a knock on the door. A little girl, aged
about nine, appeared, carrying a steaming mug. She
looked at Delyth doubtfully. 'French people have coffee for breakfast,' she said. 'But my Dad said it's un-
civilised and he thought you'd prefer tea.'

'He's right,' Delyth said, reaching happily for the mug. 'I'm Delyth. What's your name?'

'Delyth's a funny name. I'm called Ruth. If you want to get up and put on your dressing-gown you could drink your tea on the terrace. Other people are out there.'

It seemed a good idea. She rummaged in her case for a robe, then followed Ruth out of the French windows. That special sun, found only in the south, warmed her at once. In front of her was a path, a parapet and beyond it a sweep of fields. She turned right to where she could hear voices, and there was the terrace, set with white metal tables and chairs, and beyond it an incredibly blue pool. Everywhere there were flowerpots, glowing with the reds of fuchsias and geraniums.

A little group of people were sitting together—Val and Tom, a couple of middle-aged smiling men and James. They stood as she approached. 'I think I'm going to enjoy myself here,' she said.

On the table was a plate for her, a choice between crusty bread or croissants, pots of tea and coffee. She was introduced to the two men, Alan and Claude, who were water-colourists, having three weeks' holiday. 'We've been coming here for five years now,' Claude told her. 'I'd retire here if I could.'

Breakfast apparently was usually a leisurely affair. There was another guest, a middle-aged lady called Marie Brown, who had left early to go for a walk. But the others sat and talked, in no great hurry.

After her mug of tea she decided to change to coffee. It was real French coffee, strong and black. 'This must be a better heart stimulant than adrenaline,' she told James.

It was the second day she'd done it. She was getting used to sitting opposite him at breakfast. She liked it. They felt comfortable together. 'It's good for you,' he told her. 'And I know you've got a heart like a horse. Did you sleep well?'

'Wonderfully well.' She looked at the hills around them. 'And this place is so beautiful. I want to see what's behind those hills. Look, there's a village perched right on the crest over there.'

He smiled at her enthusiasm. 'I'd like to see around myself. When I'm not working we'll explore together. But first I've got to get to the hospital. See you at suppertime.'

Only then did she notice that he was in semi-formal dress. A tie was looped loosely round the neck of his white shirt, there was a blazer on the chair behind him, a briefcase by his side. She'd almost forgotten he was here to work.

'At suppertime, then,' she said, feeling rather neglected. She wanted him to herself.

He must have noticed her disappointment. 'Val and Tom will show you round,' he said. 'You still need to rest, you know.'

'I'll show Delyth round,' a small but fierce voice butted in. It was Ruth.

'Of course you will. She'll like that,' James said. He stood, rested his hand on her shoulder a minute, then walked decisively to his car.

Val drew her chair closer. 'You're convalescing,' she told Delyth. 'Take things gently for a fortnight. I've heard a bit of what you've been through, and my dear brother-in-law isn't usually very easy on his younger staff. When you've had another coffee I'll show you around the building. Then why don't you sunbathe for a while?'

Sunbathe? How long had it been since she'd had a chance just to sit in the sun? It had been years! 'I'd like that,' she said.

'Good. Have you brought any sunblock?'

Delyth looked at her, amazed. 'I never thought of that.'

'I'll lend you some. And a straw hat. Don't let it fool you around here. It might be nice now, but the weather can be a killer.'

She loved Les Cabines. Val, Ruth and Tom lived in a house on one side, the rest of them in a vast converted barn. On the ground floor there was a kitchen, a central dining area with one long oak table, bookshelves against the white roughcast walls. There were five bedrooms and bathrooms. Two open staircases led up to a large room with a polished floor and different conversation areas.

'We want guests to treat the place as their own,' Val said. 'In the kitchen there's always bread, fruit, wine, and you can make your own coffee or tea. Breakfast and lunch are largely serve-yourself, but we like to have a big meal together at suppertime.'

'Have you been here long?' Delyth asked.

'Six years now. We don't advertise any more, we get so many repeats. Michael said he'd put some money into the original conversion if we'd keep some places for his medical staff. The local hospital is pleased too. We've had quite a few medical students doing their elective here.'

For a minute Delyth felt a bit of a stick-in-the-mud. She had done her elective in the cottage hospital near home. Still, Alun had helped her so much, and she had learned a lot.

Ruth had been skipping by their side, showing Delyth things she might have missed, obviously pleased to be helping. 'Can I ask a question?' she asked Delyth.

'Of course you can.'

'Is Dr Owen your boyfriend?'

'Hush, dear,' chided her mother. 'You don't ask people questions like that.'

'Well, he seems very fond of her,' Ruth pointed out with inexorable logic. 'I think he would have kissed her this morning, but there were people watching so he just squeezed her shoulder.'

'Ruth, you don't say things like that.'

'It's all right, Val. Ruth, he's my boss, and I like him a lot, but he's not my boyfriend.'

'I'd bet he'd like to be.'

'Ruth! You must not make personal remarks. Tell Delyth you're sorry!'

Delyth saw the little face crumple. 'It's all right,' she said gently. 'There's no need to say you're sorry. In fact, we're very good friends indeed.'

This time it was Val who looked at her.

She had an easy day. She read, lolled by the poolside. Only when she tried to swim a couple of lengths did she realise how weak she was. There was a lunch of fruit and salad with Val and Tom, and then she dozed on a lounger Val made her pull into the shade. 'I told you the weather was deceptive,' she said, and when Delyth felt the heat in her skin she realised this was true.

She'd packed a set of medical textbooks but, instead of improving herself, she decided to read for pleasure. It was years since she'd done so. In the bookshelf she found a remembered joy from her childhood, Jane Austen's *Pride and Prejudice*.

'It is a truth universally acknowledged, that a young man of good fortune, must be in want of a wife.' Hmm, Delyth thought, but read on anyway.

Ruth seemed to have adopted her. She wasn't a nuisance, but was ever ready to fetch fruit or a drink. 'You can shout for me if you want anything,' she told Delyth. 'And will you tell me how to become a doctor?' Delyth promised she would.

James came back earlier than expected. She sat up on her lounger to greet him, not really surprised at the joy his presence brought her. Then she remembered the keen eyes of Ruth, and tried not to be too obvious. 'Had a good day?' she asked.

'Very good. It's a super little hospital. But yesterday is taking its toll so I came back early. That pool looks good!' His eyes moved down to her, now clad in shorts and T-shirt. 'So do you,' he added softly, and she blushed.

Before she could say anything more he went to his room, then came out in shorts and a towel, and dived in the pool. He was a good swimmer, fast but not too splashy.

As Delyth watched him complete a dozen lengths she remembered what he'd said about this particular job. It was part of a scheme to introduce British doctors to European hospitals to look at different methods of working and training, perhaps see if any ideas could be adapted. If Britain became a full member of the European Community, there would be far more movement of doctors. This scheme would make it easier.

With a lithe movement he pulled himself out of the pool. Towelling himself, he came to sit by her. She had seen his near naked body before, of course, in the race and also…but she wouldn't think of that. But each time she had been impressed by the tautness, the leanness, the sheer excitement of him. No fat, just long slender muscles, a faint dusting of hair on his chest and— A few drops of water from his rapidly towelled head splashed on her shoulders, and it felt as if they burned her. Concentrate!

'How was your day?' he asked.

'Easy. I tried to swim but I could only do two lengths.'

'You're still not fully fit,' he told her. 'Over the next fortnight you must—'

'Thank you, Doctor.' She held up her hand to stop him. 'I now know how bad I am and will follow a sensible graduated programme to restore myself to full health. I won't over-exert myself if you promise not to tell me not to.'

'Women doctors. Should be an all-male profession.'

'I want to be a doctor,' said a small indignant voice, 'and I'm a woman.'

'This is my ally,' Delyth said smugly, hugging Ruth.

'I am truly sorry,' he said. 'I apologise to both you ladies.'

The evening meal was an occasion, and a very enjoyable one. They all—including Ruth—sat at the great oak table. The lady walker, Marie Brown, had returned. She was in her fifties, a collector of wild flowers. James sat opposite Delyth. Somehow Ruth had managed to sit next to her and Marie was on the other side.

After a few minutes' casual conversation Delyth discovered that Marie was more than a collector of wild flowers—she was an expert on the therapeutic use of herbs. They had a fascinating conversation. 'Did you know that some country folk knew about penicillin years before it was discovered?' Marie asked. 'Not as such, of course, but they knew that putting some moulds on wounds might cure them.'

The meal was wonderful. There were carafes of the local wine on the table. After a cold vichyssoise they had pork casseroled in prunes, with a few simply steamed vegetables. Apparently the region was famous for prunes, and Delyth determined to take some back. Dessert was a traditional French *crème caramel*. The food was served slowly, an acknowledgment that conversation was as important as food.

After the meal Ruth was taken to bed, and with the coffee Tom gave everyone a tiny brandy. Delyth was about to refuse, but James said she should take it. It was like liquid gold, again a local brand. 'I must take some of this back,' she said, 'for my family and for a doctor who's helped me a lot. James, are you going to take some back for anyone?'

She didn't quite understand his answer. 'Yes,' he said thoughtfully. 'I'll take a couple of bottles back for a young doctor I quite admire.'

It had been a wonderful day, but at the end of the meal James saw that Delyth was tired. 'I'm feeling the strain, too, a bit,' he said. 'I think we both need to sleep. I'll come back early tomorrow again and if you like we'll do a little local tour. Perhaps a walk by the river or a couple of villages?'

Her heart caught. 'I'd love that,' she said.

Yesterday had been wonderful, but today was one of those magic times. Delyth knew that inconsequential memories were often the strongest. She remembered that time she had read about what was needed to become a doctor and had realised, I could do this. She remembered earlier, when she'd been a tiny bridesmaid for her sister Bethany, and had been firmly convinced that all that ceremony had been for her. She remembered being an anxious teenager, helping her doctor friend Alun Roberts, and an old lady patient had said, 'You've got lovely gentle hands, dear.'

Today was different. Perhaps James wouldn't remember—but she would.

He picked her up just after lunch. Said they wouldn't drive too far—there was no need to. First they walked along the sandy shore of a fast flowing river, then they drove up to a village perched on the crest of a hill. They walked along the rampart, inspected the church, smiled at the village priest. Then they went to a café and sat on the terrace. It overlooked the village square, and in front of them was a fountain. Somehow the splashing sound made the afternoon even more complete.

She looked at the old stone buildings, felt the warmth of the sun on her face, smelt the southern sun never experienced in England. James ordered himself an iced beer, and for her an odd French herbal drink, slightly alcoholic and very refreshing.

She knew she looked well. Her yellow sundress showed as much of her as she thought proper. Her hair flowed in a great train down her back, secured only by a scrunchie. Ruth had brushed her hair industriously after she had shampooed it.

He looked good too, wearing brown twill trousers, brown sandals and a plain white T-shirt. A simple cheap outfit, and in it he looked gorgeous.

'You look pensive,' he said. 'Tell me what you're thinking.'

Perhaps she was still ill and it stopped her from thinking of the consequences of her reply. Perhaps it was the sheer wonder of the day. After all, it was the kind of question that demanded a flippant answer. She didn't give one. She was completely honest.

'I was thinking,' she said, 'that if I am never happier than I am now, I will be content with my life.'

When she looked at him she realised he recognised how much she had felt that reply. He reached over the table, stroked her hand.

'I presume part of your happiness is being with me?'

She didn't speak, merely nodded.

'You know that that is the kind of remark that demands a serious answer. Delyth, at the moment I don't think I can give it.'

'You could try,' she suggested tentatively.

He paused, a long, long pause. 'You know that means making comparisons with what I felt for Erin and for Hilary,' he said, and instantly she was horrified.

'James, I didn't think. I'm sorry. I didn't mean to…'

He leaned over to kiss her, a light butterfly kiss but on the lips. 'Delyth, the past must be part of the present, but it doesn't overwhelm it. You're good for me.' His voice hardened. 'Since…since I thought I had found happiness with one woman, and then another…and then lost both, I decided happiness for me wasn't with a mate. I've told you, I look for friends, casual love affairs, satisfaction in my work. I don't know if I can, if I could…'

It was her turn to kiss him on the lips. They were salty but sweet. 'Hush,' she said, 'this is a lovely drink, a gorgeous afternoon, wonderful surroundings. I'm with you and I'm happy. I think you feel the same. I'm sorry I started us both thinking. Let's just be and enjoy. And you can start by kissing me again.'

'All right,' he said, and did. The surprising thing was, she knew she was right. The afternoon was as happy as it had been before. And she knew he was happy too.

They drove to another hilltop village and walked hand in hand through it. Down a side street was a curio shop, given half to tourist attractions, half to junk. They went in to browse, there was nothing much that interested them. Then he picked up something from the floor, and said, 'I'll buy this for Megan.'

She looked at it—a piece of cast iron with a face on it, half ugly, half disturbing. 'Megan would like that,' Delyth said, 'though I don't. You know my sister's tastes, don't you? But why buy her something?'

'Because I like her a lot.'

'I told you she warned me against you. Said she couldn't read your face.'

'She did that out of love for you. That makes me like her the more.'

She watched as he paid for the piece and had it wrapped. Then they walked to another set of ramparts, and read an account of how the village was once fortified, had been attacked and had repelled a small army, though with great loss of life. Now the landscape in front of them was beautiful, serene.

He said, 'Once real people like you and me stood here, saw enemies coming to attack their village. How d'you think they felt?'

It was an interesting question. 'Frightened, of course,' she said. 'And perhaps…it made them think more honestly about things.'

They paced on further, both, she thought, quite happy. Then, abruptly, she asked, 'I want your medical opinion. I had an injury to my head. Am I completely recovered?'

'My medical opinion?' His voice was surprised.

'Imagine I've come into one of your clinics. You've got my case notes. Am I completely recovered?'

'Not quite. Physically you're a bit below par. Your wrist has been redressed, it's a bit stiff but you can use it. Mentally you're perfectly competent.'

'Thank you, Doctor, I agree with your diagnosis. I

asked you, by the way, for your sake not mine.
Remember when we nearly made love, and you turned
me down, partly because I was a virgin?'

His answer was hoarse. 'You brought this up,
Delyth. I would never have done so. Yes, I remember.
It was one of the hardest things I've ever done in my
life.'

'Good,' she said complacently. 'I'm looking forward
to tonight's meal. I enjoyed last night and I'll go to
bed early again. Your room is next to mine. I'm going
to come to it when everyone is in bed. This is my
decision, what I want. You haven't pressured me in
any way at all.' She looked at him curiously. 'You do
want me, don't you?'

His face was half stricken, half elated. 'Want you!
Delyth, I—'

'Well, you can always lock your door.'

By mutual assent they stopped and gazed across the
fertile green valley. Then she took her hand out of her
pocket and showed him three silver foil packets. 'I
bought these on the boat,' she said. 'They're for us.
I'm not getting pregnant while I'm still training. Take
them.'

They stood like two stone statues for a moment.
'Why have you changed your mind?' he asked.

'When I was locked in that cellar I thought I might
be killed. I thought about all the decisions I'd made,
all the things I hadn't done. And being with you was
one of them. I've thought about it quite a lot since.
Now I know what I want.' She nodded at her still out-
stretched hand. 'Are you going to take these?'

Then he reached out. 'I'll take them,' he said.

They drove back to Les Cabines. A mile before they arrived she put her hand on his arm. 'Can we stop here a minute?' she asked.

He pulled onto the grass verge and looked at her questioningly. She kissed him quickly. 'I want you to know that I loved what we nearly did last time,' she said, 'and I want tonight to be as good. I'm coming to your bedroom and I only ask one thing—that you say you want me to.'

'Oh, how I do,' he muttered, pulling her to him. 'Delyth, I do. But I'll come to your—'

'No. This is my decision. I'll come to you.'

Perhaps because the night had been sorted out in her mind, she enjoyed the evening. What was to come had been decided. There was another magnificent meal, but with different people to talk to. She sat between Alan and nearly Claude. It was nearly Claude because somehow Ruth had managed to insert herself next to Delyth again. She didn't say much, was quite happy to listen. Delyth liked her.

After the meal Ruth went to bed and they played silly but enjoyable word games. Then they all went to bed. Her heart beating, she changed into her nightie and sat in the darkness waiting till the bumps and footsteps outside were silent. She waited another ten minutes. Then she padded into the hall and tried James's door. It was open. She slipped inside the dark room.

Their two rooms were at one end of the barn—there was no chance of them being overheard. Like her, he had French windows at the far end of his room, and had drawn the curtains back. By starlight she could see

him sitting on the bed. He was mostly shadow, but
there was the gleam of arm and thigh. He was naked,
and it seemed entirely proper.

She pushed down the shoulder straps of her nightie,
waited till it fell in a soft pile at her feet, then stepped
forward. Now she, too, was naked. 'I've been waiting
for this,' she told him. He stood to fold her to him, the
feel of her skin against his exquisite. But as yet he
didn't hold her tightly.

'Delyth, are you sure you want us to…? I mean,
nothing has changed and I…'

So she pressed forward and leaned against him, feeling her breasts against the muscles of his chest. 'Stop
talking,' she ordered. 'I know what I want…what we
want.'

Her words were all he needed. His mouth found hers,
and now he pulled her to him. She felt her nipples grow
proud as they rubbed against the fine hair. For a moment they stood crushed together, then he relaxed. 'No
hurry, no hurry,' he whispered. 'We have all the time
in the world.'

He eased her down onto the bed beside him. With a
small sigh of comic relief she realised that his bed was
also a double. She lay there, content to wait and to
wonder.

'You're beautiful,' he murmured, 'so beautiful.' His
hand stroked her, just the softest touch of fingertips,
from her chin, across her breasts, the gentle rise of her
stomach to the warm places below. The breath caught
in her throat at that, and he heard her alarm. 'Don't
worry,' he reassured her, 'we have time, so much time.'

So she lay there as he continued his gentle caresses,

feeling her body relax under his hands. She was afloat in a sea of sensation, her entire world nothing but the warmth, the comfort of his touching. I could lie here for ever, she thought.

After a while she wondered if she was being selfish. Tentatively, she put out a hand to stroke his neck, the rounded shoulders. Her fingers grazed his nipples and he sighed. He likes that as much as I do, she thought. Greatly daring, she moved her hand downwards and he groaned as she clasped his erect manhood.

'I didn't hurt you, did I?' she asked, alarmed.

His voice was thick, but amused. 'No, you didn't hurt me, Delyth. In fact, quite the opposite.'

Now he leaned over to kiss her. Instinctively, she knew what to do. She wrapped her arms around him, pulled him over her. First there was the delicious weight of his body on hers. Then, when she was quite ready, she opened herself to him. 'My love, my love,' he panted, and there was the briefest moment of discomfort for her. It didn't last long. He was gentle with her and soon she found herself moving with him with a rhythm that was automatic, and easy to follow. She felt the impetus of him growing, her own body writhed beneath his, and then suddenly, like a shock for both of them, they came together in a climax that had her moaning in delirious joy. 'My darling,' he muttered.

She didn't care, she stayed with him through the night. It was so good to feel his sleeping body next to hers, feel the swelling of his chest as he breathed, the warmth of his breath. He lay on his back and she on her side, one arm and one leg across him, only a sheet covering them. When he turned, his arm slid round her automatically, and she loved it.

They woke early, and he made love to her again. Afterwards they lay together, happy in each other's arms. There was an hour before they needed to rise, but neither wanted to sleep.

'Are we going to do this again?' he asked.

'Don't think I'm going to let you go now,' she answered. 'We'll do it every night while we're here, and then when we're back in London.'

She felt his body stiffen with unease. 'I may not be in London for ever,' he pointed out.

Quickly she kissed him. 'I know what you're thinking. You're going to say that I must remember that, although you're very fond of me, this is only an interlude. I must remember that you travel light. There's a chance you might be offered a job in America. If you are you'll take it and leave me behind. Isn't that true?'

He winced. 'I wouldn't have put it quite as baldly as that but, yes, I was thinking something like that.'

'Don't worry. I know that's what you're thinking.' Her voice was quite calm.

He sat up, looked down at her face on the pillow, pulled gently at the long hair that flowed over her shoulders. 'And you're quite happy with that?'

She had to get this right. 'I should be sorry to see you go, but even sorrier if you felt guilty about it.'

He was still obviously uneasy. 'Delyth, I don't want you to think... I don't want you to delude yourself and take advantage of that.'

She also sat up, and hugged him. 'Listen,' she said cheerfully, 'I'll spell it out for you. If you want to go to America, then I'll be very happy for you to go. And if you want to stay with me, then I'll be equally happy. Does that set your mind at rest?'

'After a fashion,' he said, looking puzzled. 'Because I know that you mean it. But I don't understand it.'

'You don't need to.' She glanced at his bedside clock. 'Come on, time to get up. You can go first in the bathroom and I'll sneak back next door.'

He dragged on his robe, stole one last kiss and went out.

She lay back in bed, her arms behind her head, a contented smile on her face. Who knew what the future would bring? But it was better to have James Owen for a while than never at all.

He decided not to go into hospital until later. Instead of showering, he fetched his kit from the car, changed into it and shouted to Delyth through the bedroom door that he was going for a run.

'Why the sudden change of plan?' he heard her surprised voice ask, but he didn't answer. He wasn't quite sure.

There was comfort in the accustomed exercise. As usual, he stretched first, then set off up the narrow country lane at his usual easy starting pace. To each side of him the fields and woods of Aquitaine stretched out, scenes which normally would have entranced him. Not today.

He was warm now, and he increased his pace. The slap of his feet on the gravel grew faster. There was exhilaration in the physical pain—in the gasping of his lungs, the acid burn in his calves and thighs. For a while he held it, then slowed to a speed that was fast but endurable. Now he could think. What should he do about Delyth?

There had been two terrible episodes in his life, and after them he had sworn to himself that never again would he put his happiness solely in the hands of one woman. He wouldn't risk that kind of pain again. And his life had been fulfilled enough. There had been gentle love affairs, in which neither party gave or expected too much.

But now Delyth was giving him so much. He knew already that he couldn't just walk out of her life. She was becoming necessary to him. He...he *loved* her. It was the first time he had acknowledged the fact. Bitterly he made himself say it out loud. 'I love her.'

Now what? He couldn't just overturn the way of life, the mind-set that had kept him reasonably happy for the past six years. He knew that Delyth was deceiving herself. She didn't want a temporary love affair. Ultimately she needed—she deserved—a full commitment. Could he—did he want—to give it?

There was no answer. He sprinted again, looking to the physical pain to hide his mental turmoil.

CHAPTER TEN

DELYTH accepted James going for a run without question. They had breakfast together, she waved him off to work, then wiped the sweat from her forehead.

'It's going to be hot and it's going to be sticky,' Val told her. 'Shall I make some iced fruit juice?'

Delyth told her that would be lovely. She looked at the sky—dirty grey-yellow clouds covered yesterday's sun, but it was much, much hotter. She was glad she could sit here in shorts and light shirt.

The fruit juice was refreshing, but any cooling effect was temporary. Soon she was hot again, and the box of tissues she fetched quickly emptied as she wiped her brow again and again. There was no sitting in the shade—the heat was all-invasive.

She had to think. There was a chair facing the fields and then the long line of hills. She'd sit there and hope the peace of the landscape would calm her fretful imaginings.

She'd meant what she'd said to James. He could go to America if he wanted, but she hoped that ultimately he wouldn't want to. She loved him. Because she loved him she had invited him to her bed—that was what lovers did. If they did part then she would have had something of him.

Lord, it was hot. She felt lethargic but restless at the same time. She fetched her book and more juice, but couldn't settle to doing anything. Ruth came to talk to her and say goodbye for a few days. She was going to stay with friends in one of the valleys.

'We'll all feel better when it rains,' she told Delyth. 'It doesn't stay like this for too long.'

'I'm glad. Where are you going?'

'I'm going to St Martin—it's a lovely village. Lots of places to explore.'

Val joined them, agreeing with her daughter. 'She's in and out of everyone's house,' she told Delyth. 'It's the way they are there.'

Delyth just couldn't face lunch. She waved goodbye to Val and Tom as they drove off with Ruth, then just sat waiting. She swam for a while, but had less energy than usual, and when she climbed out of the pool the air seemed thicker than ever.

She sat, trying to read. After a while a flash in the distance caught her eye. She looked up to see lightning playing round the hills in the distance. There were sheets of it, flickering like nothing she'd ever seen in England. It was beautiful to watch. Then, for the first time all day, a cool breeze came up.

Alan and Claude returned early. 'We just couldn't work,' Alan said. 'It was too sticky and we've been here before—we know what's coming.'

'This is Aquitaine, the watery place,' said Claude. 'Would you like a coffee?'

To her surprise she found that she would. 'You'd better come under the verandah too,' said Alan. 'Won't be long now.'

It started to rain. First there were just occasional heavy drops, landing on the paving stones with a loud splat. Another stronger and cooler breeze rose, then the rattling drops turned into the downpour proper. Now she felt comfortable, better than she had all day. With the others she sat under the verandah, sipping coffee, exhilarated, watching the rain.

She had been in storms like this in England, but usually after a few minutes it either stopped or slowed. Here the rain was relentless. After a while she felt subdued by the sheer power of it. 'Good thing Les Cabines is on a hill,' Alan said. 'There'll be flooding in the valleys.'

Delyth was glad to see James come home—he'd phoned to say he'd be late. She watched him pull his coat over his head and sprint the few yards to the verandah. 'Lots of road accidents today,' he told her. 'This rain after the heat of the past few days makes the roads very treacherous. I've done a couple of abdominals and a crushed chest this afternoon.'

She followed him to his room and watched as he pulled off his damp clothes. Then she hugged him. 'I'm looking forward to being in bed with you,' she told him. 'And I know we're in France but I don't want to feel as if I'm taking part in an old-fashioned French farce. It's silly, hopping between bedrooms like a couple of teenagers. I want to move in with you.'

'It's your reputation,' he said with a grin. 'You know there's nothing I want more.'

'I'll fetch my cases now.'

They joined the others on the verandah—people enjoyed looking at the rain. When asked, James described the operations he had performed that afternoon. 'The chest had been crushed by the steering-wheel—it's a very common condition. If they'd seen what I see, more people would wear their safety belts! Anyway, I cut through the ribs on the left side and found…'

His audience was enthralled. Delyth had forgotten how fascinated people could be by medicine.

Afterwards she told him, 'I'm starting to miss work now. I think I've nearly recovered. Could I come into the hospital with you, have a look round, perhaps do a bit? After all, I am a doctor.'

He laughed. 'Rest for another day, but after that I see no reason why not. Take it easy at first.'

They had another enjoyable evening meal. Tom prowled around upstairs, looking for leaks, and was pleased when there were none. James wanted to be in hospital very promptly the next day so they went to bed extra early. Their love-making was as joyful as ever. Throughout the night she kept waking, happy in his arms, and listened to the rain thudding down outside, as implacable as ever.

By lunchtime the next day it still hadn't stopped, and she was beginning to feel depressed. Val came over and said the forecast wasn't at all good—the rain looked like lasting for some days to come. 'It can really rain hard here,' she said, looking worried, 'and it's exceptionally bad about every five or six years. This might be that time. They've done a lot of flood control work recently so things should be all right. But you never know. This isn't what you want for your convalescence.'

In the afternoon she accepted a lift from Alan and Claude, and they drove down to the nearest big village.

They ran through the rain to admire the church, and then went to a museum of country life. Alan pointed out old photographs of the village, just recognisable under three feet of water, with boats being rowed up the main street.

'I hope all this flood control works,' he said.

They rushed back to the car and drove over a bridge that crossed a stream, a tributary of the main river. She remembered it when they first came, a pleasant little brook. Now it was grey and greasy, well up the banks and running fast. She shivered. This was an odd country, too many extremes. In Wales, you usually knew what to expect.

When they returned to Les Cabines Val told her that James had phoned. Today he'd be back very late—there had been a lot of emergencies. She sat with the others for the evening meal but didn't eat much. She wanted to eat with James when he arrived. The constant rainfall was now depressing the others. It was noticeable that there wasn't the same cheerfulness as the previous night.

He didn't get in until past ten. She didn't mind—no one knew better than she what medical emergencies were like. He was obviously tired when he arrived so she fetched him a meal, having told Val that she'd look after him.

'I'm earning my keep,' he told her. 'I've been operating most of the day, cases that would normally be shipped to Toulon. But they're under pressure too. How fit d'you feel?'

'I'm fit enough for work,' she told him, 'and my French is just good enough to get by.'

He shook his head. 'I want you to assist me in Theatre. That will free a French doctor. But I think you're not quite fully fit yet so you're only to work a moderate day.'

'Fine, I promise,' she said. 'But won't there be problems with insurance or something?'

'This is an emergency. The French are great at cutting red tape when they want to. There'll be no trouble with you working.'

The theatre at the Villeneuf hospital wasn't quite as well equipped as those in her own hospital, Delyth discovered next day, but she was surprised at how easily she slipped into the regime. The instruments were the same—she recognised the names of many of the manufacturers. Quickly she realised that many of the technical terms were the same. The only different thing was that the coffee was of a much higher quality. Many of the staff spoke to her in English, and most of the doctors there seemed to have some knowledge of it. She felt at home.

It was good to watch James operate again. In spite of her strapped-up wrist she was able to assist, and she knew she was a real help to him. In the morning they had a man with a case of pyloric stenosis, the muscular exit of the stomach had narrowed because of an ulcer nearby. It was a satisfying operation, she knew that afterwards the man's condition would improve considerably. He had been losing weight, becoming dehydrated.

Later on they performed a gastrectomy, removing part of the stomach of a man who had an ulcer that just would not heal. 'There may be some unpleasant post-gastrectomy syndromes,' he told her, 'but this operation was certainly necessary.'

At five in the afternoon James said, 'Don't argue. You've finished for the day. I've arranged with Tom to pick you up out at the front.'

'But there's more to do,' Delyth protested. 'I'm fine. I want to stay.'

'You can come again tomorrow. You know you've been a considerable help today, but I won't have you overtired.'

She felt like rebelling. But he wasn't an easy man to cross, and she knew he could be right. 'I'll be back when I can,' he told her. 'You know I'm looking forward to it.'

'OK, I'll go, then. But don't think this gives you a licence to boss me about.' She smiled to show she didn't really mean it.

He came into the barn later than ever, and she could tell he was exhausted. She fed him, then sent him straight to bed. 'I'll be with you in a minute,' she told him, 'and no sex tonight—you're far too tired. Just a hug and a promise.'

He managed to smile. 'I'm not too worried about the work,' he told her. 'In Africa I had a couple of emergencies like this. The French seem on top of things. Did you know that in France all emergencies are dealt with first by *sapeurs-pompiers*, the fire brigade? They're trained paramedics.'

She hadn't known that. It seemed an interesting idea.

Next day she helped James again in Theatre. They weren't quite so busy. Most of the time they dealt with the results of road accidents, repairing crushed and cut bodies. In the afternoon a cheery French orthopaedic surgeon came in to work with them. There was a particularly nasty crush injury to a woman's pelvis, and he reconstructed the bones while James tried to deal with torn muscles and veins. It was delicate work, and he performed it at speed.

Inside the operating theatre they were screened from the outside world, but when they came out they were again aware of the non-stop rain. They got back reasonably early. Val told them that the news was bad— there had been considerable flooding and it was thought there'd be no let-up in the rain. Things were getting serious, and the government had moved a unit of soldiers nearby.

Because of everyone's low spirits, Val had made a special effort with the evening meal. She'd cooked a duck and mushroom pie, with a blissfully light crust. There was a special effort made by everyone to cheer up. Delyth herself wasn't depressed, just the opposite. She felt she was getting stronger and ready to get back to work. Apart from that, she had James.

He sat by her at the great table, now candle-lit, drinking red wine. She leaned against him. Casually he would stroke her side and brush the long hair from her face. At night she always let her hair down—she knew he loved it.

He'd been attacking superstition again, and surprisingly had found a worthy opponent in Marie Brown. The older lady claimed there was a lot of truth in folk stories. Some so-called superstitions were quite reasonable beliefs. 'Willow was known as a painkiller long before aspirin,' she pointed out. 'Cobwebs *are* good for wounds if you've got nothing better to put on. And what about acupuncture? Even fifteen years ago it was regarded as the province of charlatans. Now many GPs practise it. It's accepted by the BMA.'

Delyth had to smile at the vehemence of the old lady, and the grace with which James accepted the force of her argument. 'You're entirely right on all of the points,' he said.

It was a more pleasant evening than they'd had for a while. 'Still an evil night,' Tom said. 'I think we'll have a special treat. I'll fetch the brandy from the house.'

He came rushing back. 'Just caught the telephone,' he gasped. 'James, will you come and take it? An emergency—sounds a really bad one.'

The two men ran out. No one round the table spoke, waiting for what was to come. Then James returned, his face set.

'Big trouble,' he said. 'They need all the doctors and nurses they can round up. They know I've had some experience in disaster management.'

He turned to Delyth, not as a lover but as a coldly assessing doctor. 'You've been ill. Are you fit enough to work all night, perhaps outside in rough conditions? Give me an honest answer—this isn't a test. You'll be worse than useless if you collapse or something.'

'I'm fit enough,' she answered frostily. 'I'm not a man, letting testosterone talk for me.'

He gave her a grim smile. 'That's what I thought. Get dressed in rough clothes, boots and anorak. Bring a complete change in a bag—you might get wet through. And put your hair up. We'll be picked up in five minutes.'

The others clustered round him, asking for details, but he didn't seem to know much. When she had changed they all went outside onto the verandah. It was dark, still raining. In the valley they saw the smudged lights of a vehicle coming towards them.

Eventually it splashed into the courtyard. It was a large van with great wheels. On the sides were fastened spades, drums, a ladder, tools that might be needed in a rescue. With James she jumped into a cramped little space, already nearly filled by men in canvas overalls and helmets. Then James was deep in conversation in French with the senior man there. There wasn't much chance for her to attend. She had to hang on grimly as they bumped and rolled onwards. The driver wanted to get somewhere in a hurry. And the rain pelted down.

They drove for perhaps three quarters of an hour. Towards the end she knew they were climbing, presumably a narrow road—she could tell by the straining engine, the difficulty in getting round corners. There was the odd glimpse of overhanging trees, steep banks. Finally they stopped. The man in charge snapped out a series of curt orders. The others seemed to know instantly what to do. Delyth followed James, her hood up against the rain.

They stepped out and heard the rattle of generators, saw great arclights among the trees, a huddle of vehicles. There were two great tents so they ran towards them.

'All this has been set up in the past two hours,' James said. 'I'm very impressed. This is the first staging post. There will be relays of ambulances, taking people down to hospital. We'll also take the young and the old. Lots of people won't need hospital attention, but they'll be cold, wet, miserable and perhaps shocked. We've to get them warm, get food in them, reassure them and find them somewhere to sleep. Then they'll survive. People can die in situations like this, not because they're seriously injured but because they've not been looked after.'

He pointed to one of the tents. 'There are campbeds in there, blankets, a mobile kitchen. But we triage everyone in this tent. You might be acting as a doctor, but you're more likely to be needed as a nurse and auxiliary. That OK?'

'Fine by me. I'll do what's necessary.' She was excited to be working with him again. 'But, James, what exactly has happened? I don't know.'

'Sorry! It's all happened so fast. There's a village in a valley just below us. Above it were two dams, old ones. The lower dam broke its banks because the upper one was over-full. The water was funnelled down the valley, and a wall of it smashed through the village. Many of the houses were knocked down and some people are trapped. Everyone is being evacuated. We've got army engineers looking at the top dam—they think that might go too. It's bigger, and if it breaks what's left of the village will be just flattened.'

Somehow, she knew. 'James, what's the village called?' she asked.

He frowned. 'St Martin.'

'That's the village Ruth is staying in with friends. She's here somewhere. James, we have to find her!'

* * *

There was no place for personal feelings in disaster management. Neither James nor Delyth could look— that was the job of another team. James promised he would make enquiries but she knew that her anguish would have to be contained. She was a doctor with a job to do! She was taken into the larger tent and introduced to a doctor who fortunately spoke excellent English. 'My name is Etienne,' he told her. 'Later perhaps we may become acquainted. Please help me with these new arrivals.'

She was impressed by the efficiency. Although it was a tent, they were on a hard floor, there were examination couches behind screens and trolleys with instruments. She was found a white coat.

As Etienne spoke a group of wet, mudstained people were ushered in. Orderlies separated them into male and female, helped them out of wet clothes, gave them blankets and offered hot drinks. Delyth noticed an old lady who seemed bewildered by what was going on. She would be her first patient.

With a nurse, she helped the old lady undress, then conducted a quick examination. It wasn't a good sign that the lady neither commented nor objected, but limply let them do what they liked with her. She had been wet through, but although it wasn't too cold it had been sufficient to produce hypothermia. Delyth guessed that her patient's core temperature was below 30 degrees. But she wasn't shivering.

The nurse quickly recognised what was wrong. After wrapping the old lady in blankets, she rushed to fetch a silver space blanket to wrap around them. The old lady's body temperature should now slowly come back to normal. It was important not to warm her too quickly. The nurse now seemed happy. Delyth was not. Something was wrong. Summoning what little French she had, she said, *'Diabétique?'*

The nurse looked at her curiously, and then realisation struck. She went to question the other people who had come in. There was a flurry of French, and the nurse returned to say, *'Oui, diabétique. Pardon, madame.'* She shouted something and a moment later the old lady was swept away on her stretcher. Recovering from hypothermia when diabetic, that was much more tricky. She would need careful management.

Nothing much else was exciting, though she was kept busy. There were cuts that needed cleaning and a couple that needed careful dressing. She also irrigated the eyes of a sobbing woman who had fallen in the mud with her eyes open. Delyth carefully rolled back the upper and lower lids, then, using her ophthalmoscope, she looked for signs of scratching or injury. There were none. The woman, now much quieter, was given soothing drops.

There was a lull, then in came a young soldier, a field dressing pressed to his forearm. Delyth lifted it to look—a nasty deep cut made by something sharp. She and the nurse cleaned the cut, then Delyth sutured it. The soldier stared stonily ahead. When she had finished Delyth called for Etienne, who, she could see, wasn't busy.

'I think this boy should rest for a couple of hours before he starts work again,' she said.

'I agree entirely.' Etienne spoke rapidly to the boy, but she couldn't follow what was being said—only that the young soldier was agreeing. Then the nurse put on a thick dressing, and the soldier walked to the tent door. But, instead of turning to the rest tent as he had been directed, he turned the other way.

Etienne shrugged. 'I could report him to his senior officer for disobeying orders,' he said, and winked at her.

A smiling man came round with a great mug of coffee. It smelt wonderful. Looking at her watch, Delyth saw that she had been working for four hours. Time was passing. She forced herself not to think of Ruth. James had said he would make what enquiries he could—she would just have to wait and hope. She had noticed one or two cases carried by stretcher straight into a curtained-off area. They were the dead. She shivered.

There were fewer cases now. She had time to chat to her nurse, whose name was Monique, even sit in a chair. She went to peer into the section of the tent where the more serious cases were being dealt with. They, too, seemed to be working less frantically. Etienne smiled and waved. She looked outside. It was still raining. It seemed less dark; dawn was breaking.

Then James came out of the darkness towards her. He was dressed in overalls, like the others, and wearing high boots and a helmet. He was covered in mud, and his face looked more tired than she'd ever seen it before. He looked defeated. She felt a great rush of love for him. She herself was dog-tired. She wondered how long it would be before she could shower, and they could tumble together into his double bed. But there were other questions first. 'Ruth?' she asked, and agony lanced through her when he shook his head. 'She's missing.'

Etienne had also come to the tent door. After another swift exchange James said, 'There's not so much work for you here now. I want you to come with me. There's a job...just for you.' She thought he sounded uncomfortable. But Etienne shook her by the hand, thanked her and said he hoped they would meet again soon in happier circumstances. Monique kissed her. Then James was walking her quickly towards a waiting Jeep.

'Tell me about Ruth,' she said. 'What does "missing" mean? Is she...is she likely to be dead?'

They climbed into the Jeep, and it eased forward. 'In a situation like this,' James said, 'one of the first jobs is to ask everybody where they were, and who they were with when the water hit. That way we can crosscheck that everybody has been found. In fact, we fetched two old ladies out of a bedroom a couple of hours ago. They'd slept through everything. But Ruth had gone out to visit friends. She didn't say which ones—she was friendly with everyone—so we don't know where to look. She's the only one unaccounted for.'

In spite of the rain it was getting lighter now, and Delyth could distinguish trees alongside them. 'Where are we going?' she asked.

'We're going to the village of St Martin.'

The road was precipitously steep, and she winced as she thought of the drivers who must have negotiated these evil bends. Then the Jeep stopped where a few other vehicles were parked. James and Delyth climbed out. They went to the edge of a cliff and below them was the village of St Martin.

Through its centre raced a stream, obviously usually small but now the size of a small river, carrying debris including small trees. She could see where the flood had hit—buildings had been knocked down and those houses still standing had their ground-floor doors and windows knocked out. There were groups of men searching.

'The whole village will have to be rebuilt,' said James, 'perhaps in a more sensible spot than below two old dams.' He led her to the largest vehicle and they looked into what was obviously a command post. There was a radio, sheets of papers, supplies.

James talked rapidly to the man in charge. The man looked worried, shook his head, tapped his watch. He glanced at Delyth. 'Fifteen minutes,' he said. 'Fifteen minutes *justement*.'

Delyth looked at the whiteness round James's eyes, saw the channels of pink skin where sweat had trickled through mud and dirt. Her heart went out to him, he looked so desperate. He took her by the arm, and when he spoke she could tell he was near collapse. 'The army engineers say the top dam will go at any time. It will certainly flatten anything that's left. In fifteen minutes he's ordering his men back up here. Very properly, he won't risk their lives.'

He grabbed her other arm and pulled her round to face him. 'Ruth is the only one left unaccounted for. Perhaps she's already dead. But something tells me she's still alive and still in the village. She's trapped, and she's going to be killed.'

'Something tells you?' she asked flatly.

'Something tells me. I can't get it out of my head. I want you to come down there with me, see if this...power you've got can find her. The men just don't have time to search everywhere. And it's too wet for the dogs.'

She stood still in the rain, looking at him in horror. It was the last thing she had expected.

'It just happens,' she said. 'I can't turn it on—it just happens. Sometimes not for months.'

His shoulders sagged. 'Of course,' he said. 'Silly of me to ask. Will you wait for me in the car? I'll be with you soon.'

'No. I'll come down and do what I can. But don't...don't rely on me.'

They slithered down to the village main street and waded cautiously over the bridge which had not yet been swept away. He walked just behind her but didn't speak or touch her, except to steady her when she stumbled. She walked to the top of the village main—and almost only—street, turned and looked downwards.

She didn't know what to do. On her left was what had once been the Café des Sports. Now its windows were smashed, the pillars at the front bent. Water had raged through the single room, tumbling chairs and tables together against the far wall, and above them there was still a calendar advertising Pernod. She shivered, but forced herself to walk over and step inside the room.

Forget her fatigue, forget her discomfort, forget the noises around her—the shouts of the searchers, the roar of the river, the rattle of water dripping on the floor, the creaking and groaning of the building. Where was Ruth? She tried to empty her mind, to think as—'Delyth, move!' It was her own name being shouted in that agonised way. She heard the bang of James's feet on the floor, felt his arm round her waist and was half thrown, half carried out of the wrecked building. Together they fell, sprawled in the mud outside the café.

There was the shriek of bending wood, then a series of sodden thumps. She twisted to look behind her. The front of the café had collapsed. Where she had been standing, a giant beam had smashed through the floor.

James's face was only inches from hers. Even through the mud she could see that it was stricken, ashen-white. 'Delyth, you could have been killed,' he muttered. 'You could have been killed. What would I have…?'

Adrenaline flushed through her system—she wasn't tired any more. She knew it was the fight-or-flight syndrome. In about half an hour her body would react and she'd feel worse than ever. But not yet. She scrambled to her feet.

'We've got work to do,' she snapped. 'We've got to find Ruth.'

She watched as he fought to gain control over his feelings, to put behind him the horror of what had just nearly happened. He stretched out his arms, flexed the muscles of his neck, clenched his fingers into fists then relaxed them. 'Yes, we've got to find Ruth,' he said, in a voice she barely recognised. 'Delyth, you've got to find Ruth.'

She turned and walked down the main street. She

had never tried to turn on this power, didn't know how. Instead she thought of herself as a little girl aged nine, obviously bored after days confined because of the rain. What would she do? What would she think? Where would she go? But now she would be cold, frightened, probably wet, perhaps even injured. She hadn't shouted, had she? Or if she had she hadn't been heard.

She tried to empty her mind, to be a little girl, cold, wet, frightened. Cold, wet, frightened. She slipped, gashing her hand on a protruding spike. She didn't notice the pain but stuck the hand in her pocket. She was in a different world. She was a little girl, cold, wet, frightened.

Once or twice she stopped, gazed blankly at a building, then moved on. Behind her James walked, not allowing himself to think or hope. Then she stopped and rocked on her feet. He put out a hand to steady her, then withdrew it. She pointed. 'There,' she said.

She pointed to an ancient building on the bank of the river, now half under water. Once it had been a washplace for the entire village. Now it was long since abandoned. But behind it was a storeroom, with a door no more than four feet high. The side had been collapsed by the river.

James turned and shouted, and a four-man team ran towards them. Delyth watched wide-eyed as they seemed to take an awfully long time carefully prising open the door. 'Quite often the act of opening a door makes more of the building fall down,' James told her. 'You might know that now. But these men are well trained.' He slipped his arm around her shoulders.

The door opened a little. One man peered round it

and shone a torch. Delyth heard him shout. James's grip on her tightened and she found she had to make herself breathe. No, she didn't. She knew that someone was living, breathing, inside that storeroom.

Two men managed to wriggle inside, then there was a long pause. One of the other men was carrying a radio. It suddenly crackled. He listened and then turned to hold out five fingers. Five minutes left.

'All the men are ordered back,' James said tautly. 'The dam won't hold out for long.'

One of the men backed out of the storeroom, carrying with infinite caution a limp form in a pink dress, with blood down one arm. From somewhere a collapsible stretcher appeared. Ruth's motionless form was laid on it. Delyth stood back as James made the swiftest of examinations, stuck a field dressing onto the injured arm, then stood back to let the others wrap a space blanket around the little figure.

The four set off at a jog trot, the stretcher between them. James and Delyth followed. They saw the other groups moving out, too. She had to lag behind when they reached the steep climb out of the village. James held her, encouraged her. They watched the fitter soldiers race ahead to place Ruth in the waiting ambulance.

The ambulance didn't move before they got there. Instead, James went inside to conduct a more detailed examination. Delyth sat on the steps outside. A kindly soldier took out a space blanket and wrapped it around her shoulders.

'Come in,' James called after a while. She climbed into the ambulance. Ruth's eyes were open.

'Hello, Delyth,' she said. 'You found me. I knew you would.' The eyes flickered shut and she slept.

'Nothing seriously wrong,' James said, 'but I'll ride in with her. I'll arrange for you to get a lift home. A night in a hospital bed for Ruth and she'll be fine.' Delyth bowed her head and wept.

She woke as the Jeep stopped at Les Cabines. A soldier half carried her to the verandah. Lights were on and a little group of people was waiting. Marie put her arm round Delyth. 'We've all been up all night,' she said. 'Val and Tom heard about Ruth just after you'd left. They heard she'd been found half an hour ago and they've gone to the hospital. Apparently, you found her?'

Delyth shrugged. 'There were a lot of people looking,' she said. She was more tired than she'd ever been in her life before. She couldn't think, couldn't make decisions, couldn't cope.

'I know what you need,' Marie said, and half dragged her through the barn to the bathroom. Delyth let the older woman undress her and ease her into a warm bath, smelling of something aromatic. She accepted a cup of tea with sugar in it. And after a while she felt a little better. Still tired, but she could think.

She managed to get herself out of the bath and pulled on her nightie. 'What about James?' she asked Marie.

'When that young man of yours appears I'll put him in the bath, then into bed with you.'

'Let him undress himself,' Delyth advised, and staggered into James's room. There was so much to think about and she wasn't going to think about any of it.

Outside it was still raining. Her eyes shut the minute her head touched the pillow.

In the middle of the night—or possibly the middle of the morning—she felt someone climb into bed with her. She felt warmth against her back, an arm round her waist. She smiled, and went back to sleep.

Eventually, she woke. Something was different. She squinted at James's bedside clock. Half past one. She must have been very tired. What was different? Then it struck her—the silence. No constant drumming on the windows and the veranda roof. It had stopped raining.

Beside her was James, still fast asleep. He was lying on his side, his arm above the sheet. She ran her finger from his wrist along the muscles of forearm and biceps to his rounded shoulder and his neck. He slept on. So she kissed his shoulder, and still he slept. Less sleep than she'd had.

Without disturbing him, she wriggled out of bed and put on her robe. Peering through the window, she saw a weak sun, the first for days. She walked to the kitchen.

Alan and Claude were there. 'Everyone's asleep,' Alan explained. 'Last night—this morning—was hard on everyone. Are you all right now, Delyth?'

'I'm fine now. But last night took it out of me.'

'You can tell us all about it later. Sit there, I'll make you a drink. Tea or coffee?'

'Coffee, I think, and make it strong. Can I have two mugs?'

She took the coffee on a tray back to the bedroom.

After glancing in the mirror, she pulled a comb through her hair. In the night it had come undone. Then she slid in beside James again. The rich aroma of coffee filled the room, and after a while a voice from the pillow said, 'That smells good. Is there one for me?'

'If you want to sit up.' He did. She looked at his tousled hair, unshaven face, sleepy expression. 'You look a mess,' she said, 'but I love you. Here's an early afternoon kiss.'

'You don't look a mess,' he said in reply. 'You look incredibly beautiful, and here's a kiss back.' His took longer.

'Drink your coffee,' she said after a while. 'You must need it. Er...how's Ruth?'

'She's good. Val and Tom are with her. She's shocked and scared, but there's nothing seriously wrong and they'll probably discharge her tomorrow. She's only alive thanks to you, Delyth.'

'Coffee, I said! We can be serious later when you've woken up.'

So they finished their coffee and then he fetched more. He climbed back into bed. 'If we're going to be decadent we'll do it in style,' he told her. 'We have to talk.'

'Sounds serious again. It was a hard night. I'm not sure I want this right now.'

'I've heard that you can't have everything you want in this life.' His smile took the sting from his words. 'But I think I can. Delyth, I want an honest answer. I told you I would only have a temporary affair with you. I tried to be fair with you. But you came to bed with me anyway. Was it because you thought that I didn't mean it?'

Her reply was reflective. 'I just didn't know, James. But some time with you, even a little, was better than no time at all.'

'So it wasn't this feeling, this voice you have, that told you to do it?'

'No. And before you scoff, you have that feeling sometimes too. You knew Ruth was in that village last night, didn't you?'

'Possibly,' he sighed, 'or possibly I just wanted her to be there. Tell me, how did you find her?'

'I just imagined I was a little girl. Where would I hide or play? And then it just came to me.'

'So it wasn't something…something paranormal?' His voice was eager.

'Yes, James, I think it was,' she said gently. 'And you think the same.'

'Perhaps.' He was silent a moment, his face suddenly sombre. 'Too much happened yesterday, Delyth. I'm still trying to get it in order in my mind. D'you realise you were nearly killed?'

She had forgotten! 'I suppose I have to thank you,' she said slowly. 'You pulled me out of that café just in time. But I was concentrating on…' Realisation suddenly dawned. 'You saw it happening again! First Erin, then Hilary, then me… What did that nurse call you? You thought you were the Angel of Death?'

He smiled. 'You're alive, Delyth. No, quite the opposite happened. In that split second I realised that all the good things in life have to be grabbed. I'd be an utter fool to let something as miraculous as you escape me. Tell me, seventh daughter of seventh daughter, what do you foresee for us?'

'I don't need any paranormal powers to tell me that. It's a choice that only you can make. Perhaps I'm taking things for granted, but I think we could have a happy life together. You've had more than your share of misery—now you could share in happiness. You've got a ready-made family. They'll love you and I know you'll love them.'

'You're going too fast,' he told her. 'Wait a minute.' But then he realised he didn't want to wait a minute. He took one, two, three deep breaths. 'Delyth,' he said, 'will you marry me?'

She didn't need to think about her answer. 'Of course I will,' she said. 'I couldn't imagine loving anyone more, couldn't think of anyone who would make me more happy. Come here and kiss me.'

She slid down the bed, her long hair coiled on the pillow. 'I've got a thought for you, James. I'm the seventh daughter of a seventh daughter. Supposed to have powers. What if we have seven daughters?'

'So long as they are all like you,' he said, kissing her again.

#1 *New York Times* bestselling author

NORA ROBERTS

brings you more of the loyal and loving,
tempestuous and tantalizing Stanislaski family.

Coming in February 2001

The Stanislaski Sisters

Natasha and Rachel

Though raised in the Old World traditions of their
family, fiery Natasha Stanislaski and cool, classy
Rachel Stanislaski are ready for a *new* world of love....

*And also available in February 2001 from
Silhouette Special Edition, the newest book in the
heartwarming Stanislaski saga*

CONSIDERING KATE

Natasha and Spencer Kimball's daughter Kate turns her
back on old dreams and returns to her hometown, where
she finds the *man* of her dreams.

Available at your favorite retail outlet.

Where love comes alive™

Don't miss the reprisal of
Silhouette Romance's popular miniseries

**When
King Michael of
Edenbourg goes
missing,**

his devoted
family and loyal
subjects make it
their mission to bring
him home safely!

Their search begins March 2001 and continues through June 2001.

On sale March 2001: **THE EXPECTANT PRINCESS**
by bestselling author **Stella Bagwell** (SR #1504)

On sale April 2001: **THE BLACKSHEEP PRINCE'S BRIDE**
by rising star **Martha Shields** (SR #1510)

On sale May 2001: **CODE NAME: PRINCE**
by popular author **Valerie Parv** (SR #1516)

On sale June 2001: **AN OFFICER AND A PRINCESS**
by award-winning author **Carla Cassidy** (SR #1522)

Available at your favorite retail outlet.

Where love comes alive™

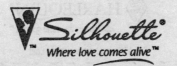

It's hard to resist the lure of the
Australian Outback

One of Harlequin Romance's
best-loved Australian authors

Margaret Way

brings you

Look for

A WIFE AT KIMBARA (#3595)
March 2000

THE BRIDESMAID'S WEDDING (#3607)
June 2000

THE ENGLISH BRIDE (#3619)
September 2000

Available at your favorite retail outlet.

NEARLYWEDS

Almost at the altar—will these *nearlyweds* become *newlyweds*?

Harlequin Romance® is delighted to invite you to some special weddings! Yet these are no ordinary weddings. Our beautiful brides and gorgeous grooms only *nearly* make it to the altar—before fate intervenes.

But the story doesn't end there....
Find out what happens in these tantalizingly emotional novels!

Authors to look out for include:

Leigh Michaels—The Bridal Swap
Liz Fielding—His Runaway Bride
Janelle Denison—The Wedding Secret
Renee Roszel—Finally a Groom
Caroline Anderson—The Impetuous Bride

Available wherever Harlequin books are sold.

HARLEQUIN®
Makes any time special ™

MAITLAND MATERNITY

Where the luckiest babies are born!

In February 2001, look for

FORMULA: FATHER

by Karen Hughes

Bonnie Taylor's biological clock is ticking!

Wary of empty promises and ever finding true love,
the supermodel looks to Mitchell Maitland, the clinic's
fertility specialist, for help in becoming a mother. How can
Mitchell convince Bonnie that behind his lab coats and
test tubes, he is really the perfect man to share her life
and father her children?

*Each book tells a different story about the
world-renowned Maitland Maternity Clinic—
where romances are born, secrets are revealed...
and bundles of joy are delivered.*

HARLEQUIN®
Makes any time special ™

Silhouette®
Where love comes alive ™